STRANGE IDEAS: DEATH, DESTINY AND DECISIONS

LOUISE WEST

Copyright © 2013 Louise West

All rights reserved. This book may not be reproduced in any form, in whole or in part, without written permission from the author.

ISBN: 1482033755

ISBN-13: 978-1482033755

DEDICATION

For all of those with strange ideas who dare to dream.

For Rob & Mary,
I hope you enjoy my strange ideas!

Louise
xxx

CONTENTS

A FLIP OF THE COIN	1
STAMP	21
ROCK GOD	69
SUPERSTITION	97
LATE: A GHOSTLY TALE	135

ACKNOWLEDGMENTS

This book wouldn't have come together without help from some very special people. Much love (and cake) to Tori and Nan, for inspiring me, Kirsty, Lucy and John for devouring my drafts and being honest but helpful, and my wonderful, supportive family for putting up with endless conversations about plots, characters and overuse of adverbs.

Also, I'd like to apologise to the people who I have asked some apparently peculiar questions of in the name of research. Hopefully, you'll see that it was worth it.
Yes, Becky, Sally and Jess, I do mean you.

A FLIP OF THE COIN

He hadn't expected it to be like this.

The harsh fluorescent light reflected painfully from the sterile green walls and stung his watery eyes, causing him to squint through his eyelashes. The scent of bleach and flowers tried, but failed, to mask the underlying odour of defecation and death. He wasn't sure what he had expected. A hand, warm against his cold and paper-thin skin, held his own gently, dutifully. After a long and interesting life, James Edward Bailey waited for the end, not with fear or trepidation, but with patience. At least he was not alone.

The silence was heavy, broken only by his own laboured breathing and the rhythmic tick of a cheap plastic clock on the wall. A countdown. He wondered how many minutes he had left, how many aching inhalations and exhalations. Not many. The shadow of pain in his chest told him that. He turned his head to look at his silent companion, unmoving and bent over his withered hand. It wasn't anybody he recognised. He wondered if his children had visited, wondered if they would visit. He hadn't seen them for a long time.

The figure sensed his movement and raised its head. A

man. His face was pale and tight, but kind. His hair, like his eyes, was dark and soft. He met his gaze and smiled weakly at the stranger. He wondered who he was, and why he was here with him. He moistened his dry lips and spoke.

"Do I know you?" His voice sounded weak and frail, like it had no life left. He remembered when it had boomed. The stranger shook his head.

"No, Jimmy, but I know you." He laid his other hand over Jimmy's and his fingers stroked soothingly as he answered; they were bone-thin but comforting. Jimmy imagined his skin whispered like sheets of parchment where they touched. "I will be here for you."

"That's very… kind of you."

"It's what I do." The stranger smiled. Jimmy searched through his foggy memory for any recollection of his face. The morphine had numbed his brain. He remembered when it had been so sharp. He couldn't place him.

"What is your name?" Jimmy wheezed.

"I have many names. Some call me Thanatos, some the Grey Walker, others Anubis." He paused and looked directly into his eyes. "I imagine you would know me better as Death."

Jimmy gasped, a rattling sound that vibrated through his frail body. Was this some kind of joke? He peered at the stranger's pallid, drawn face and knew that it was not. Death had come for him.

"I've never been much of a believer," Jimmy began. Death smiled again.

"I know. I know everything about you. I know everything."

Jimmy didn't know whether he found that comforting or not. He shifted slightly and tried to sit up. He couldn't. He remembered when he had been so strong. Death made hushing sounds and shook his head.

"Relax. It won't be long now. It's almost time."

Jimmy let his head fall back onto the pillow. His heart, weakened by time and cigarettes, tapped quickly in his chest. He wasn't sure what he had expected. His visits to church had been limited to obligatory weddings, christenings and, more frequently in the last years, funerals. He didn't believe in God, or Heaven. He'd had no time for religion. Not like his Emily.

He smiled as he thought of her. *Emily.* His beautiful wife. His one loyal supporter. They'd met in an office where she'd been a secretary and his firm the suppliers of their office furniture. She'd given him an ear-bashing over a chair that had broken when she'd sat on it and he'd invited her out to dinner to apologise. They'd been married three months later, when the spring blossom fell from the trees like the confetti that no one could afford.

He'd never really recovered after her death four years previously. He'd sat by a hospital bed like this one, watching her fade away before his eyes, feeling a flame inside him gutter and perish. He seldom cried, but he had wept that day, knowing she was gone forever.

"Will I see her again?" he asked Death. He didn't have to say her name; Death knew who he meant. He gestured to the other side of the bed.

"She's here now."

Jimmy turned his head as quickly as he could manage, and his eyes opened wide in wonder. To his right, radiant with youth and love, sat his Emily. Her golden hair was thick and lustrous, and her skin glowed a soft pink. Her lips formed a smile like a rose blooming as she took his hand and pressed her cheek to it.

"Jimmy," she sighed. "I've waited so long for you to see me again." She raised her head and beamed at him. Jimmy whispered her name as he strained his fingers to grasp hers more firmly, wincing automatically as the slight movement tugged the plastic tube that fed him morphine through his bruised and collapsing veins, surrounded by mottled and dry flesh. He tore his eyes away and back to Death.

"I was wrong? About the afterlife? There *is* a Heaven?"

Death shrugged.

"Of sorts. People make their own Heaven. And Hell."

"Which one will I go to?"

"That depends."

"On what? On whether I believe?" Jimmy began to feel desperate. "Because I do! I believe!"

"It's not that simple." Death withdrew his hand from Jimmy's and reached into his pocket. Jimmy noticed, for the first time, that Death was wearing jeans and a hooded jumper. He wasn't sure what he had expected. Death's hand returned, wrapped tightly around something small. He stood and stretched out his arm, holding his closed fist in front of Jimmy's face. From the corner of his eye, Jimmy noticed Emily's brow crease anxiously.

Death opened his fingers slowly. A shiny silver coin gleamed on his upturned palm, its edges smooth from aeons of handling. The markings on its face were unfamiliar to Jimmy.

"What is that?" Jimmy whispered, confused.

Death turned the coin gently in his fingers, the otherworldly metal catching the light as it moved through his powder-soft fingers. The effect was hypnotising, and Jimmy had to force himself to tear his eyes away from it in order to scrutinise Death's impassive face for an answer. Death curled his fingers tightly around the coin and fixed his soft eyes on Jimmy's before he spoke.

"This coin has decided many events, some that affected the lives and fates of millions, some which were significant to only a few." The shadows under his eyes darkened, as if weighed down by the past. "Its decision is final and irreversible. Its judgement is always absolutely fair and unarguable."

Emily shivered, the tiny vibration tingling against Jimmy's skin where she grasped his hand. He broke away from Death's gaze to look at her. A single tear drop gathered, poised to fall, even as she smiled bravely for him. Jimmy suspected he knew where Death was going with this. He turned back to face him, waiting for him to continue.

Death hadn't moved an inch. When he had Jimmy's full attention once more, he pocketed the small coin.

"When the time comes," he said, "This coin will decide your fate."

"That's it? My… fate… depends on a random chance?" Jimmy was horrified. He hadn't believed in an afterlife until five minutes ago but, now that he knew there was one, he was damn sure of which way he wanted to go. He trembled with outrage. "That's preposterous!"

"It is the way it works. It cannot be avoided." Death spoke calmly, a barely-perceptible regret in his task masked by his composed demeanour.

"But what about people who have led good lives?" Jimmy wheezed in protest. "The Christians, the charity workers, the children? Are you saying that an innocent child may be condemned to Hell on an arbitrary gamble?" A flicker of his old fire returned, and he gasped a breath before continuing. "And what about murderers? If I do go to heaven, am I expected to sit at God's table with rapists and dictators?" He fell back onto the hospital pillow, exhausted from his outburst.

Death held up his hand in supplication.

"Let me explain," he said. "This coin is fair, but it is not unbiased. No one person, even a child or a murderer, is either completely innocent or evil. People are not so two-dimensional; they are many things; they present many faces to the world. We are all ultimately judged by our thoughts and deeds. So it will be with you."

Jimmy was confused. His morphine-addled brain struggled to formulate sense from Death's words. Was it random or not? Could he have any say in this, or was his afterlife to be decided by a flimsy piece of metal?

"I don't understand. I thought you just flipped that damn coin."

Death nodded, running his thumb over the coin's surface, polishing it with his skin.

"I will. But before I do, we will consider how it will be weighted."

Jimmy pondered this for a moment before responding. If the coin was weighted, surely that gave him a better prospect?

"So I do have a chance to affect the outcome?"

"No. In the respect that your life has been lived, that it is almost over, there is little you can do to change the weighting now. But you will at least see and understand how the judgement has been made."

Jimmy didn't see how that was any comfort.

"So if I have lived a good life, the coin will land in my favour?" he persisted.

"Usually," replied Death. "It is, after all, a coin, and subject to natural laws- as all things are."

"Still sounds like a damn fool way to make decisions to me," Jimmy muttered. Death cocked his head to the side and narrowed his eyes slightly. Jimmy wondered if Death had anything to do with the weighting. He hoped not. There was a long, uncomfortable silence before Death spoke again.

"There is an alternative," he said finally. "You may choose not to let the coin decide at all. If you wish, you may choose oblivion, in which case your afterlife will cease to be an option. It will be nothing. No Heaven, no Hell. Oblivion."

Jimmy looked over at his Emily. She was every bit as beautiful as he remembered, every inch of her perfection. She smiled supportively, as she had always done every day they had been together. How could he pass up the chance to spend eternity with her? He skimmed quickly over his life. He was sure there had been more good than bad. If he had a fighting chance, he had to take it. He turned back to Death.

"I choose the coin."

"You will accept its decision? There is no going back once the coin has been flipped."

Jimmy swallowed, a nervous lump in his throat.

"Yes."

"Good." Death pocketed the coin and settled himself more comfortably on the chair. "Then it begins. Tell me about your life, Jimmy."

Jimmy shifted uneasily under Death's heavy gaze and the thin layer of blankets. This was like some sort of horrendous interview. What was he supposed to say? How much time did he have? He weighed up his options and decided to play it safe: start at the beginning.

"Well, I was born in 1935, in a seaside town on the south coast."

"Yes, I know that already."

That was obviously the wrong way to approach this. He looked pleadingly up at Death, hoping for a clue. Death relented and threw him a bone, as it were.

"Tell me about your mother."

"She was a hard-working woman- always busy, hardly sat down for two minutes." Jimmy smiled as he remembered her. "She used to read me bedtime stories every night, and let me lick the spoon when she'd been baking."

"Were you kind to her?"

Jimmy searched his memory. There'd been the odd row, mostly when he was a teenager, where he'd said things he hadn't meant and had swiftly regretted. He always gave her his house-keeping money on time, and when he'd married Emily and settled in a house of his own, he'd visited regularly to see she wasn't lonely. In her final years, when she couldn't manage the house on her own, he'd paid through the nose for her to be cared for in a fancy nursing home.

He frowned as he remembered how she'd cried that day, leaving the house that had been her home for so many years. She didn't understand, couldn't see that it was for the best. In the end, he'd become impatient with her sobs and had practically marched her to the car. He hoped that wouldn't count against him. In his own way, he'd been distraught that day too, watching the woman who had represented strength to him weaken and crumble so. He couldn't bear it. Emily had held him that night as he lay, silent and brooding, picturing his old mum's tear-streaked face as he'd left her in the home, all blank walls and sparse furniture, surrounded by boxes filled with her old life.

The memories faded and he was back in the room. Death waited patiently for his answer.

"I... yes, I was kind to her. I did my best. She never wanted for anything."

"Correct." Death smiled. "You cannot be blamed for old age and infirmity: these things are beyond the control of mortals. You feel regret, but your mother's life was happy: you made her happy. She loved you very much and she understands now why you did what you did."

"How do you know all this?" Jimmy asked, bewildered.

"She told me just now, while you were considering your answer." Jimmy followed Death's gaze. His mother stood by the bed, smiling sweetly down on him, just as she had when she was tucking him up for the night when he was a child.

"Hello, Jimmy love," she whispered.

"Mum?" Jimmy could barely get the word out. She moved

silently around the bed until she stood by his head. She laid her hand on his brow. Her skin smelt of lemon verbena and clean sheets. He breathed the scent in greedily, ignoring the pain in his chest. How he'd missed her. Death allowed them a moment before pressing on. Jimmy fought the urge to look at the clock on the wall.

"Your sister. Tell me about her."

Jimmy's heart sank. Deborah. They hadn't spoken in years, not since she'd shamed the family by running off with a sailor. He remembered the last time they'd spoken- well, argued. Anger prickled under his skin at the memory. He pictured her, painted lips and swollen belly, spouting nonsense about this so-called love she'd found. *Love?* he'd spat at her. *What does a floozy like you know about love?* Hurt had crossed her face at that and, at the time, he'd been glad. He'd banned her from his house, insisted that she was never mentioned in his presence, and destroyed every scrap of her existence in his life.

Sometimes his decision sat heavy in his heart. He'd heard of her death weeks after she'd passed, too late to attend her funeral, not that he was sure he'd have gone anyway. He wished it could have been different, but his pride had prevented him from reconciling with her, even after her death. He couldn't take back the words he had said, so it was easier to ignore them- and her.

His emotions played across his face like a film and Death watched every scene in thoughtful silence. Jimmy raised his chin as best he could, defiant.

"She shamed the family! What was I supposed to do- be *pleased* that she'd thrown herself into the gutter and dragged us down with her?" Despite his fiery words, he knew Death noted the tremor of doubt in his voice. Death gestured with a tilt of his head to where Deborah now stood, lips painted and belly swollen, exactly as she had looked the last time he'd seen her, right down to absence of a ring on the third finger of her left hand. Her expression was sorrowful as she shook her head slowly, pitying him in his pride and anger.

"Jimmy," she sighed. "You never did understand. Henry was the love of my life- I was incomplete without him. We saw the world together, we raised a family, and every day of our long years together was filled with laughter and joy. Our love was strong and pure, even though we didn't start off in the respectable way." She raised her hand to stop Jimmy's interruption. "I wish you could have seen how happy we were together- you'd have known it was the right thing for me to do. You'd have liked Henry, if you'd have just given him a chance."

From the corner of his eye, Jimmy saw his mother nod in agreement.

"It wasn't right, what you did," he replied. "Getting in the family way, unmarried- the shame of it! The scandal! And running off, leaving me and Mum to face the neighbours; I was angry, Debs." His face twisted at the memory. "You abandoned us. Dad was barely cold in his grave- we needed you there."

She bowed her head in acknowledgment. "I know it seemed selfish- maybe it was. But Henry offered me a fresh start, a new life." She stroked her bump tenderly. "New life," she repeated. Jimmy was aware of Death's gaze, scrutinising him closely. He couldn't lie; Death knew everything somehow. He turned to him, his thin voice almost pleading for understanding.

"I was angry," he repeated, as if that explained or excused everything. "I couldn't..." He considered his choice of words carefully; this was important. "I *wouldn't* forgive what she did to us." The words stuck in his throat; he never had been very good at admitting when he was wrong. Emily squeezed his hand in support; she knew how hard this was for him. "But maybe I should have... for Mum's sake." His mother looked down at the floor and shook her head. Deborah sighed. Death said nothing. Jimmy felt the weight of words unspoken pressing down on him.

"Let's move on." Death spoke smoothly, but Jimmy knew he had failed this test. He was stubborn- he admitted that- and proud; these traits would surely count against him, weigh the coin unfavourably. He hoped he would have another chance to redeem himself. He looked at his wife and mother, silent by his side. Longing swelled his heart; he wanted to be with them again, to be with his loved ones in Heaven. He had to keep trying.

"What- or who- do you want to talk about next?" he asked hoarsely. Death waved his hand and another figure appeared next to his sister. He was dressed in a shabby-looking suit, the elbows worn shiny by years of propping up bars. His sparse hair was combed neatly back in ribbons of white, the lightness contrasting with the sullen rings under his eyes. Jimmy stared into his weary face and knew him. Neville Cooper, his first business partner. He looked much older than Jimmy remembered, broken, as if the world had crushed him. Jimmy struggled to think; had he caused him to be this way? He didn't think so. They had gone their separate paths long ago. His memory was so hazy now, like little lights were blinking out. He smiled tentatively at the tired-looking man. Neville gazed back, his face cold and stony.

"Neville, how have you been?" Jimmy stopped himself- was it appropriate to say that to the deceased? "I often wondered how you'd got on, after we..." Recollection flooded his brain like water breaking through a dam. Neville continued to stare hostilely as Jimmy's memory filled with the manner of their parting.

"You wronged me, Jimmy."

Jimmy opened his mouth to defend himself but, in his

heart, he knew the words were true. He and Neville had been friends for a long time; they were at school together, played cricket together, got into the usual boyhood scrapes together before Jimmy had gone to work for Neville's father at his workshop.

Bert, a gruff-looking man who stood no nonsense from either his son or his friend, had worked them hard and trained them well. When he decided to retire, he had named Neville and Jimmy as his successors. Jimmy knew this had rankled with Neville, who believed the family business should be his alone, but they had glossed over it at the time, as friends do. Except their friendship had never been the same after that. Jimmy had sensed the jealousy creeping into Neville's heart; he didn't understand his father's decision, didn't see why he had to share what should have been his alone. The old man had been insistent, however; he understood that Neville needed Jimmy's quick wits and hard-bargaining to ensure the business continued to flourish. And flourish it did, due to Jimmy's sharp business sense and Neville's gift for craftsmanship. Everything was perfect, but for Neville.

Neville changed after his father's death. He began to drink heavily and brood over what he perceived as his father's betrayal of his only surviving son. He made mistakes, became sloppy; the broken chair that had brought he and Emily together had been one made by Neville. Jimmy found it increasingly difficult to work with him, so twisted had Neville become in his hatred, so careless and unreliable. Snide comments about who should rightfully own the business escalated quickly into full-blown arguments, the two of them nose-to-nose on the workshop floor, in full view and hearing of the junior employees. The situation, and their friendship, deteriorated from strained to intolerable. Without Neville's knowledge, Jimmy had put on his best suit and visited the

A FLIP OF THE COIN

bank manager. He returned with an offer- take the money and leave.

Neville had been furious. He'd refused, as Jimmy had suspected he would, so Jimmy had been forced to hit Neville with the alternative.

"Fine," he'd said coldly. "I'll leave then. I'll leave and set up on my own." He gestured out of the office window at the workers, busily crafting furniture. "But I'll tell you this-" He'd leaned in close to Neville's face, ignoring the broken veins and reeking breath to stare straight into his eyes. "-I'll be taking that lot with me. Do you think they'll stay with a drunk? A man who wastes his talent by hitting the bottle every hour he's awake?" He'd thrown the contract on the table and left.

It hadn't taken long for word to spread. Neville was on his doorstep within the week, a pathetic mess, the signed contract in his hands. His staff had made it quite clear with whom their loyalty lay. Jimmy didn't gloat; enough of the man that Neville had once been remained for Jimmy to recall their friendship. He'd suggested, kindly, that Neville should come back when he'd sorted himself out, that there would always be a job for a skilled craftsman. He hadn't come back though. Jimmy had hoped, rather than truly believed, that he'd used the money wisely and set up somewhere new, rather than drinking himself to death.

He looked at him now and doubted his optimism. Neville's nose was swollen and red, his hands trembled and his eyes were hard as they bore into Jimmy's.

"You wronged me," he repeated. Jimmy couldn't answer. Neville had been the master of his own downfall but Jimmy was starting to realise, too late, that he could have saved him. He could have done things differently. He remembered how distraught he'd been when his own father had died- how different things might have been had it not been for his mother, firmly steering him through his grief while putting hers to one side. He'd never realised quite how much he owed to her.

He closed his eyes, resignation etched in the lines of his face. He had not lived a good life; he accepted that now. He'd hurt people. His chest ached with more than the pain of his shallow breaths. Their rasping wheeze and the ticking clock were the only sounds to break the heavy silence. He was running out of time.

Death had watched the two men silently, but spoke now.

"Jimmy, do you wish to go on with this?"

Jimmy moaned. He didn't think he could bear this anymore. To have his life played out, to be judged, to be found wanting… maybe oblivion would be better than this. He forced his eyes open, ready to tell Death he had changed his mind, but his gaze fell instead on a different figure now stood at his bedside.

Jimmy recognised him at once.

"Terry?"

Terry reached down and took Jimmy's other hand, patting it companionably.

"Yes, old friend, it's me. I beat you to it, it seems!" He laughed, the rich sound echoing around the small room. "Thanks for the flowers."

Despite his heavy heart, Jimmy grinned, his thin lips curling back in a genuine smile. Terry always had that effect on him. *Thanks for the flowers…* Jimmy never sent flowers to funerals- didn't see the point in the expense for a soul that couldn't appreciate them- a belief that Terry had ribbed him about many times. *Tight-fisted old man*, he'd teased. *Saving your pennies for a rainy day?* Jimmy had harrumphed and pretended to be offended, but no one could really be cross with Terry.

"Did you like them?" he said, a chuckle rising in his throat. It brought on a coughing fit, one that left him gasping and clutching his chest. Terry waited until it had passed, undaunted.

"You always said I'd be the death of you," he joked. Jimmy chuckled again, but more gently this time.

"I did indeed." He lay back on the pillow in order to take a better look at his friend. Terry, like Emily, seemed to glow with warmth and life. His blue eyes twinkled, like he was about to share a joke, and his beard curled in wispy tufts around the lower half of his face, his crooked teeth yellow against the snow-white hairs. He stood tall, crowding the room with his personality and physical bulk. He was still larger-than-life, even in death. "You're looking well, Terry."

"Can't complain." His friend's face grew uncharacteristically sombre for a moment. "I'm hoping you'll come and join us, Jimmy. It'd be nice to have the old gang back together."

Jimmy looked to Death for any sign that this might be the case. Death's face was inexpressive as always, giving nothing away. He prepared to speak, to tell Death about Terry, but Death instead directed his next instruction to Terry himself.

"Tell me how you met Jimmy." The eyes of everyone in the room moved to rest upon Terry, who beamed proudly, seemingly ignorant of the weight his next words would have.

"Jimmy found me sleeping rough in the alley behind his workshop," he began. Jimmy noticed Neville wince at the words 'his workshop' and another flicker of guilt ran through him. Terry continued, unaware of his tactlessness. "He told me to sling my hook, or words to that effect." He winked at the women. "I shan't embarrass the ladies present with his exact phrase- it being a bit fruity for delicate ears." They blushed and giggled- even Jimmy's mother. Jimmy shook his head in wonder at Terry's ability to charm in even these circumstances. Terry, encouraged, warmed up to his theme and continued. "I chanced my luck and asked him for a cuppa before I went." He grinned at Jimmy again. "I could see he was a softie, despite his tough-man act."

Jimmy remembered that day. Emily, with characteristic shyness, had announced her pregnancy just the night before, and he had floated off to work the next day, whistling cheerfully like the leading man in a romantic film. He'd been on top of the world that morning.

"You were just lucky you caught me in a good mood," he grumbled, trying to hide his smile. Terry laughed at him, not fooled at all.

"I didn't just get a cuppa- I got a job," he grinned. He looked to Death to explain further. "I'd been laid off, got booted out of my digs- but Jimmy could see I was a good man. He gave me a week's trial, and let me sleep in the office. I worked hard, learned fast and stayed." He laid his hand on Jimmy's again, his calloused touch warm. "I stayed for nearly twenty years."

"Only because you worked so cheap," Jimmy chuckled. He didn't worry now if Death understood their jokes. He was having fun, swapping banter with Terry. It was like old times again. But Terry spoke his next words seriously, looking straight into Jimmy's eyes, genuine gratitude in his expression.

"I was so grateful for that chance, Jimmy. You saved me," he said. "You saw beyond the mess I was in and gave me a hand up when you could've given me a boot up my-" He remembered the ladies, and stopped himself, grinning boyishly at the faces in the room. "What I mean is, you were like a father to me- I wouldn't have got myself back on my feet if it hadn't been for you." He squeezed Jimmy's hand gently. "Thanks for that, old man."

Jimmy had never known Terry speak so openly before. He was quite taken aback, but pleased. It was true- he had treated Terry like a son, been proud of his achievements. He'd enjoyed watching him grow up, fall in love, start a family.

He'd been a proud godfather to Terry's two sons too, especially after...

Ominous clouds formed in Jimmy's mind, pushing the happy memories away and filling the space with shadow.

It had been a terrible day when the phone call had come. Jimmy had been wrestling with the accounts, his bad mood not helped by the black storm clouds that threw rain at his office window. A terrible, black day. Maggie, Terry's wife, had been the one to tell him. A drunk driver. He'd blocked out the details.

The church was packed for Terry's funeral; he'd had so many friends. They'd barely all squeezed into Terry's house for the wake. Jimmy had spent most of it in the back garden, playing football with the two boys, their smart jackets rolled into balls as make-shift goal-posts, their black ties abandoned by the hedge. It was what they'd needed, and Jimmy had imagined Terry's hand on his shoulder, thanking him for keeping the boys away from the grieving adults, letting them deal with it their own way, in their own time.

When dusk began to fall, he'd taken them inside and put them to bed before returning to the almost empty living room where Emily and Maggie sat, holding hands in silence. The bouquet of flowers he'd brought for Maggie had filled the room with their sweet scent. He'd refused lilies, choosing forget-me-nots and white heather instead. *Thanks for the flowers...* He'd made sure that Maggie was alright after too, that she never had to go without. She and Emily had remained firm friends over the years, and Jimmy had tried hard to make up for Terry's absence, taking the boys fishing, teaching them how to play cricket and occasionally giving them a stern talking-to when they stepped out of line. He hoped he'd got it right, hoped he'd done it the way Terry would have wanted.

A sharp pain in his chest pulled him out of his reverie. He

screwed up his face with the effort of not calling out. Emily clutched his hand until the spasm passed.

"It's... it's not long now, is it?" Jimmy whispered. The ache spread from his chest through his whole body, dulling his senses more than the morphine had. The faces around him blurred before slowly settling back into focus. His father now stood at his mother's side, his arm around her shoulders, pulling her close. Jimmy's heart fluttered erratically, fighting for these last few minutes on Earth.

Death shook his head. "No, not long now. Remember, you still have a choice."

Jimmy craned his neck to see his father again. He nodded slightly, a tight smile on his lips as he looked down at his son, an old man in an unfamiliar bed.

"I'm ready." Jimmy's words were barely audible over the ticking of the clock, and the effort to speak them was great. He cast his eyes around the assembly, noting the new faces that had silently materialised- his next-door neighbour, the old lady he had run errands for as a boy, the man from the pub whose nose he had broken in a fight. So many faces, so many lives linked to his own.

Death stood up to deliver his summary. His face was unreadable.

"You have been a proud man, Jimmy, stubborn and often blinkered to the feelings of those around you when the personal cost to yourself was too great. Your need for security, respectability and success led you to cast many by the wayside and judge them unfairly when they did not meet your high standards." His voice boomed unnaturally around the room, echoing as if the words were spoken in a vast cave, rather than a hospital side-room. "At times, you have been cold, harsh- even cruel. You considered yourself morally above others and placed your happiness and convenience in higher regard." Jimmy tensed himself for the final blow, but was surprised to hear Death's voice soften.

"You have also shown great kindness to those you loved and trusted-" he continued, "-those you deemed worthy. You changed lives for the better, with unselfish motivations. You respected the sanctity of friendship, family and marriage, making difficult decisions in the sincere hope that you were doing the right thing."

Death's eyes burned into Jimmy's for a moment, their depths conveying a brief flash of understanding and sympathy. "I know all about difficult decisions." He looked away, the connection broken, and continued to speak.

"You valued and modelled a determined work ethic and never forgot your roots, or those who had supported you. Your determination and loyalty is to your credit. Your weaknesses came from a desire to do right by those you cared for, to be the man your father would have wished, to steer the world around you on a true and just course. You were not always correct, but your intentions were good."

Death stared into Jimmy's eyes.

"Are you satisfied with this summary?"

Jimmy nodded, mute with anxiety and weakness.

"Then it is time. Your life is ending, and the decision must be made before your last breath leaves your body. Do you wish me to flip the coin?"

Jimmy summoned the last of his strength.

"Yes."

"You understand that its result cannot be reversed? That your afterlife, once determined, cannot be changed?"

"Yes." A whisper, his last word.

Death slipped his hand back into his pocket and pulled out the coin. Jimmy looked around the room at the faces from his past and wondered if he would see them in his future. They crowded round him, all but one, laying their hands on his weak and frail body in forgiveness and hope.

Jimmy closed his eyes and uttered a silent prayer to the god he had never really believed in, before opening them and fixing his watery gaze on the coin in Death's pale hand.

Death nodded and flipped the coin high into the air. Jimmy gasped involuntarily in anticipation as it flew towards the ceiling, his hand locked tight in Emily's.

He watched helplessly, his eyes glued to the silver coin as it pirouetted, glinting as it twirled in the air, turning like a graceful acrobat as it soared then paused at the top of its arc. He barely noticed the doors burst open as his children raced in, babbling apologies about traffic and gulping back tears. His eyes followed the coin as it tumbled towards Death's white palm, turned upwards to receive the verdict, the light dancing on the surface of the disc as it descended. His own hands were filled by the living flesh of his children and the cooler whispers of loved ones long-gone. He was glad his children had come, but sad that they had not had a chance to say goodbye properly. He hoped he would see them again one day, when their time came. Seconds stretched endlessly and he held his last breath as the coin bounced on the cold hand, exhaled it in a whispered "I love you," as it twisted in the air again-

And landed.

STAMP

Ben pushed his way through the heaving, sweaty crowd and used his elbows to lever himself into a place by the bar. He was uncomfortably close to the blonde girl next to him, her rough extensions scratching against his bare elbow as she swayed and clutched the bar to keep her balance. Horse-hair, probably, he thought.

She laughed at something her friend said and flicked a thick, heavy lock back over her shoulder, catching him in the face. He flinched and tutted. She looked drunk and slobbery; she was probably about thirty seconds away from either spilling her drink or vomiting down herself. He didn't fancy either of those options. He brushed the sleeve of his best Superdry shirt unconsciously. Better to be safe than sorry; he held his breath and leaned towards her, gently nudging her along the bar in order to give himself some room. She slid with little resistance and no one rushed to fill the space, despite the throng.

The club was packed tonight. As he waited to catch the eye of one of the harassed looking barmaids, he craned his neck to look behind him. A sea of faces, flushed and euphoric, spread out across the cheap, sticky carpet and onto the dance floor. Tim was out there somewhere, probably chatting up some poor girl. Ben peeked again to his right at the blonde. She looked in her mid-twenties, but she was dressed as if she wanted to be younger. She'd probably fall for Tim's patter; she looked drunk enough. If Tim didn't get any luck he'd send him up to the bar for the next round, let him charm her. The girl belched and cackled, rubbing her hand across her face and smearing her lipstick. Ben looked away again and shuddered. Maybe not.

He waved his ten pound note at the barmaids and finally managed to get the attention of the brunette with too much fake tan. She leant forward over the bar, flashing a hint of streaky cleavage that was further spoiled by the heavy Argos-bling around her neck.

"What can I get you, sweetheart?"

"Two bottles of Becks, please," Ben shouted over the thumping dance music. The barmaid- her name badge read Tanya- smiled flirtatiously and turned away to the chiller cabinet. As she bent down to grab the bottles, she lingered just a few seconds too long and he was treated to a nice long look at her backside. He averted his eyes quickly, but not quickly enough. She straightened up and returned, pulling the caps off the bottles and placing them on the bar with a leer.

"Seven eighty, please."

He handed the note over and she took it, staring just a little too long into his eyes. Ben looked away, uncomfortable. She wasn't his type. She sauntered to the till and punched some buttons before bringing him his change. She winked, and moved on to the next customer. Ben pocketed the coins and picked up the beers.

Squeezing and shoving past the writhing bodies, he fought his way to where he'd left Tim guarding a table with a view of the dance floor. His friend was alone, bouncing his head to the beat of the music with an almost manic intensity. He nodded to Ben as he sat down.

"Took your time."

"Seriously, mate; the bar was rammed. Took me ten minutes just to get served. Nearly got molested by some bird who was getting a bit too friendly as well- you know what I mean?"

Tim nodded sagely.

"Yeah, mate- in your dreams!" He laughed and continued bouncing, pausing only to take a long drink from his bottle. His eyes scanned the crowded room, searching for vulnerable prey. Tim wasn't fussy, which was fortunate as pickings were slim tonight, if the mess at the bar was anything to go on. Too much false advertising for Ben's tastes; he preferred girls with a bit of class. He sipped his drink and followed his friend's gaze.

Bit of a mixed bunch tonight. There were the usual hipsters parked on a table in the corner, holding court and looking just too damn cool, but next to them was a hen-party: a vision of shocking pink, plastic tiaras and short skirts. He grinned as they shrieked loudly at their friend, who was dancing on the table, enjoying the look of disgust from the hipsters. Posers.

He shifted in his seat so he had a clearer view of the dance floor. A group of blokes, all obviously off their faces, were attempting to break-dance in the middle of the swarm. They had drawn an amused crowd of barely-legal girls and a couple of bouncers. It wouldn't be long before they crashed into someone or got chucked out, or both.

He continued letting his gaze roam across the faces until he found one he liked. Bingo. She was on the edge of the dance floor, away from the drunken break-dancers, dancing alone. She swayed her hips in time to the music, lifting her arms and trailing her hands through her long black hair. Her perfectly-shaped mouth formed enticing shapes as she sang along to the song. Ben swallowed. She was gorgeous.

He glanced quickly at Tim. He was lost in his own little world, bouncing away and knocking his drink back. He hadn't seen her yet. Ben looked back at the girl. She ran her hand down the side of her body and closed her eyes, lost in the music. Her skinny jeans clung to her curves like they were sprayed on with paint. Ben made up his mind.

"I'm going to go and dance," he shouted in Tim's ear. Tim nodded and grinned, making no effort to move and join him. He was probably too drunk by now.

"Good luck!" he yelled, as Ben drained his drink, stood up and made his way to the dance floor.

The song changed just as he reached the edge: a pounding bass with a sexy hook. Perfect. He shuffled his way casually over to the girl. She had her back to him and, this close, he caught flashes of the perfect creamy skin of her back and shoulders through the moving bodies. He inched closer, not wanting to seem too obvious. He elbowed some of the competition out of the way and eventually managed to manoeuvre himself so he was beside her.

She turned suddenly and stopped dancing. He stopped too, surprised at the electric jolt that ran through him as his eyes met hers. He had never seen anyone so beautiful before. Her eyes were like toffee, honey-brown and sticky: they seemed to draw him in and hold him there. She smiled, revealing small white teeth. Her smile was flawless. She began to move again, inviting him with her eyes to join her.

Their bodies swayed together in perfect synchronicity. She turned so her back was against him and her soft hair brushed against his cheek. It smelt of violets. He ran his hands over her hips and she placed her own hands on top of his, holding him there. He glanced over to Tim and was gratified to see him stood up, staring, with his mouth literally hanging open. Ben grinned back.

The girl turned again so she was facing him. Her perfect mouth opened and she asked him, in a voice so sweet it made his knees weak, what his name was. He swallowed, not sure he could remember.

"Ben," he managed to say. She smiled and carried on dancing, brushing against him every now and then. He leaned forward, partly so he could breathe in the scent of her hair again.

"What's your name?"

"Cassie." She lifted her hands and rested them on his shoulders as the song changed again to some Euro-pop rubbish. "Want to go somewhere quieter? I know a place."

Ben blinked in surprise but nodded, too awed to push his luck by speaking. She gestured with her head at Tim.

"Your friend can come too. He'd have more luck there."

Ben looked over to Tim, who had recovered from his stupor sufficiently to make rude gestures behind Cassie's back, telling him in no uncertain terms that he considered Ben's luck to be in.

"Ah, I don't know that he-"

Cassie placed a polished fingernail on his lips.

"It'll be fun. It's a nice place. Nice people." She took his hand and led him from the dance floor. "Come on."

Ben collected Tim and his jacket and hailed a taxi from the rank outside the club, his fingers still locked with Cassie's. They felt comfortable, like they were meant to be entwined together. An unfamiliar flutter tickled in Ben's chest as she wiggled closer towards him- she was something special, he just knew.

Tim, for once, was behaving himself. He couldn't resist

the odd peek at Cassie's backside though, Ben noticed. He wasn't bothered. Cassie was making it clear who she was interested in. He hoped fervently that his breath didn't smell of onions. With the hand that wasn't holding Cassie's, he tried to cup and sniff his breath discreetly. She caught him and grinned. He grinned back. Another invisible spark shot between them, making the air inside the taxi crackle with potential.

After a surprisingly long drive, away from the lights of the main clubbing strip, the taxi pulled up at the address Cassie had given. It wasn't an area of the city that Ben had visited before; he didn't even know there was a club here. It looked like an industrial estate. They climbed out of the taxi and stood outside of an unlit building. Tim looked around incredulously.

"Where is it then?" he asked. Cassie laughed, a soft tinkling sound like wind chimes.

"It's hidden- very exclusive." She led them down an alley and to a green side-door with a tacky, temporary-looking neon light above it. It blinked haphazardly, illuminating most of the letters that spelled out the name: *'Futures'*. She knocked softly and the door was opened by a huge bouncer, a man who was almost as wide as he was tall. In fact, Ben thought, looking him up and down nervously, he looked more like a wrestler than a bouncer.

"Good evening, Cassandra," he grunted. Cassie smiled and released Ben's hand to embrace the suited gorilla. Ben battled a sharp stab of jealousy as he watched the man wrap his hulking arms around her slender waist. Cassie giggled again and stepped back as he released her.

"Levi, these are my dear friends, Ben and...?" She turned her head and beamed at Tim. Ben smirked as he watched the effect her smile had on his friend.

"Uh- Tim. I'm Tim." Flustered, he held out his hand to shake Levi's. Levi looked at it pointedly and made no move to take it. Tim dropped his hand quickly. He shuffled his feet awkwardly. Cassie laid her hand on Levi's arm.

"Levi, darling. Let us in quickly, please- it's freezing out here."

Levi stepped back to let them pass. Cassie took Ben's hand in hers and led him up some narrow stairs, Tim trailing behind like a balloon.

The music hit Ben long before they reached the inner door; it was intoxicating and hypnotic. Cassie turned and smiled sweetly at him before pushing the door open into a room that swam with colour and flashing lights. It took his breath away for a moment. A wall of beautiful faces turned to greet him. He wondered if he had somehow ended up at an after-show party for fashion models. He noticed a few ordinary-looking faces mixed in between the chiselled cheekbones and heart-shaped pouts. They must be the agents and hangers-on. Maybe Cassie was a model. That would explain a lot.

He turned to look at her; she was gazing up at him as if he were a prize that she was thrilled to have won. Her golden eyes seemed to glow from within as she stared into his.

He stood, transfixed, and barely noticed when someone took his free hand. He jumped as a sharp prick of pain flared across the back of it though, and looked down indignantly at the black ink below his wrist.

"Ow- what was that for?" The woman, astonishingly beautiful in a gold dress that defied gravity and reason, smiled and waved a silver hand stamper at him.

"Members only. You need a stamp."

"Oh." Ben watched as Tim's hand was stamped. The silver hand-stamper sparkled in the flashing strobe lights, giving it an almost magical radiance. Tim rubbed his hand and swore.

The woman waved them in and Cassie led Ben and Tim to the dance floor, where Tim was immediately approached by a petite red-head in hot-pants. Waggling his eyebrows suggestively at Ben, Tim led his new friend to the bar, leaving Ben alone with Cassie. She winked at him as the music changed pace, wrapping her arms around his neck and pulling him close.

When Ben woke, his first thought was of her. He knew she'd leave before morning- why would a girl like that want to stick around in a crummy flat on the wrong side of the river? Nevertheless, disappointment sat heavy in the pit of his stomach. He thought they'd had a real connection; he'd never enjoyed talking to a girl so much before. They'd sat up for hours, chatting, flirting, sharing their ideas on life, and love. As for when the talking had finished… He rolled over onto his back and gazed around his bedroom.

His clothes were heaped on the floor where he'd left them, hurriedly, and there was no note on the bedside table. He hadn't really expected her to leave one. What would it say? *Last night was the best night of my life- call me* and a phone number? No. Whatever magic had happened last night had evaporated in the morning sun, which was streaming through a gap in the curtains in a very unhelpful way. He doubted he'd see her again. Why would someone like her be interested in someone like him?

Grunting, he dragged his tired body out of bed and into the shower, turning the radio on as he passed it. The Sunday morning show mix was soothing and exactly what his throbbing head needed. He let the hot water blast down onto his neck and reached for the shower gel. He washed himself absent-mindedly, feeling only vague annoyance that the stamp on his hand wouldn't wash off. At least it was proof that last night had been real. He gave up scrubbing it and turned off the shower.

When he was dressed he rang Tim. He didn't answer until the fourteenth ring, and sounded terrible when he did.

"Hello?" he groaned.

"Tim, mate. How's your head?"

"I've been better. How did your evening work out? You get lucky?" Even over the phone, Ben imagined Tim's eyebrows waggling.

"Good night, yeah. Top," Ben replied, refusing to be drawn into a play-by-play re-enactment. Cassie was classy. She deserved better than that, even if she had disappeared along with the stars as soon as dawn broke.

Tim was disappointed.

"Aw, mate. No details? She was fit as!"

Ben laughed.

"Get lost! No details- and I don't want to hear any details about your after-club shenanigans either. I'm feeling queasy enough as it is."

"You're no fun. Fancy a fry-up?" Ben looked at the clock on his bedside table. Just after eleven.

"Yeah, go on then. I'll pick you up."

"Cracking plan, mate. I can barely see straight, let alone drive. See you in twenty." Tim hung up.

As they ate their breakfast, and despite Ben's protests, Tim insisted on giving a full run-down of his night with Angie, the girl in the hot-pants. Other than agreeing that it had been a great night, Ben resisted Tim's attempts to discuss Cassie. He didn't want Tim knowing everything. He was almost glad when he could make his excuses and leave.

Back home, he had another go at scrubbing off the stamp with a nail brush and some white-spirit. It wouldn't budge. The line of numbers stayed stubbornly visible and fresh-looking. He tried on and off all afternoon, in between watching the football highlights and Hollyoaks omnibus he'd recorded, but it looked like it was there to stay for now. Wondering idly how long it took for skin to renew itself, he turned in early, pulling the duvet over his head.

"Boss wants to see you."

Ben started, jolted out of his stupor. He'd been staring at the screen for fifteen minutes, not seeing a single number on the spreadsheet before him. His head still ached from the weekend. He hated Mondays. In fact, he hated every day in this job. Still, it paid the bills. He looked up at Neil, his line-manager.

"Me? What about?"

"He didn't say." Neil walked away, his face expressionless.

Ben pushed his chair away from his desk and walked to the small office that was separate from the large, cubicle-filled room where the drones worked in isolated cages. He knocked on the door and Andy's voice barked at him.

"Come in!"

Ben opened the door and entered the room. Andy, his boss, was sitting at his untidy desk, tapping a pencil against his teeth. A neglected pot-plant gathered dust on the window-sill that was home to a collection of photo frames and ornaments declaring that Andy was *The Greatest Dad EVER!!!* Ben cleared a pile of papers from the chair and sat in it.

"Alright, Andy?" he said. He wondered why he had been summoned. Andy stopped tapping and glared.

"No, as a matter of fact, I'm not alright, and neither are

you. You've made a right mess of this-" he gestured at a folder containing the documents Ben had placed on the desk just after lunch "- and you look like death. I'm fed up with you rolling up on a Monday in a state. It's every bloody week, for crying out loud! Where the hell is your head at?" He paused, hoping for, rather than expecting, an answer. Ben didn't fill the silence. Andy sighed and continued, warming up to his theme.

"I was young once, I used to be out all hours, but I never turned in shoddy work. It's not good enough. If you're serious about your career, you need to take more pride in yourself than- *this*." He gestured with his pen to Ben's appearance. Ben shifted uncomfortably in his chair. His trousers were crumpled and he had a stain on his tie. He never made much of an effort for work, but he had to admit he looked particularly bad today. Andy's eyes fixed on the stamp.

"What is *that*? Is that a *tattoo*? You know our policy on acceptable presentation. What are the clients supposed to think when they see you looking like you've slept in your clothes and with a dirty great tattoo on your fist?"

"It's not a tattoo- it's a stamp from a club. It won't wash off," Ben muttered, rubbing at the offending black ink. Andy frowned.

"Then I suggest you get your backside home and into the shower- put some effort into sorting yourself out. We have a reputation- an image to project to clients- and, right now, you do not meet standards. Sort yourself out and get back here tomorrow or I'll have to seriously reconsider your suitability for our company. Consider that your official warning." He turned away to his screen. The meeting was clearly over.

Ben stood up and skulked back to his cubicle. He collected his things and left the office. A few curious glances were thrown his way but he kept his head down and ignored them. He pushed the button for the lift down to the car park level, feeling the stares stabbing his back as he waited.

He breathed out slowly once the doors closed and he descended. Andy was a jobs-worth, but he needed to keep him sweet and he hadn't enjoyed his dressing-down. Ben looked at the stamp on the back of his hand and rubbed it with his thumb. He resolved to buy some bleach on the way home, see if he could burn the thing off. Andy would flip his lid if he turned up tomorrow with it still there. He'd do some laundry this afternoon too- make sure he had a clean shirt for tomorrow. The stamp seemed to stare back at him, taunting him with its refusal to shift. Ben shoved his hand into his pocket so he wouldn't have to look at it.

That night, Ben spent a solid hour trying to remove the stamp. His skin grew sore and red from the bleach, soap, white spirit and scrubbing brush that had been applied in vain. No matter what he tried, it looked as new as it had on Saturday night. He threw the scourer -his latest attempt- into the sink and kicked the bathroom bin in frustration. What kind of freaky ink was this?

He turned on his laptop and typed *'how to remove ink'* into the Google search bar. A million results- and all of them useless unless he wanted to remove ink stains from clothes. He tried again. He typed *'ink stamp won't come off hand'* and hit search. This was better. He clicked through the first few links, but he'd tried every suggestion already- except the one about rubbing urine into it- gross.

He flopped back in his chair. This was stupid. There had been at least two hundred people in that club on Saturday night: he couldn't be the only one stuck with a freaky-ink stamp. In desperation he added *'freaky'* to his search terms and hit return again. This time, he got lucky.

He clicked on the top result that the search threw up '...*club **freaky ink stamp** and now it **won't come off**...*' and read the post. It came from a discussion thread entitled 'Futures Club stamp'. Futures? That was the name of the club where he'd been stamped! Intrigued, he quickly scanned the first entry. It was from a girl -he assumed, from the name given- who was complaining that she too had been stamped at an after-hours club and couldn't wash the ink off. He checked the date. The message had been posted two weeks ago. Her picture was highlighted, indicating that she was online right now. He skipped the advice that followed the original post and scrolled down to the comments box.

Me too, he typed. *I've tried everything I can think of. Does it wear off eventually? How long did it take?* He clicked the button marked 'Post comment' and waited. The reply came back almost immediately.

It hasn't. Going for laser removal. Ben gasped. He leant forward and typed again.

For real??? My boss is gonna kill me!!! Why won't the freaky ink wash off? What the hell did they use?

She replied quickly.

Not ink. Have you checked your numbers?

Ben was confused. His numbers? Did she mean lottery numbers? And what did she mean "Not ink"? He peered closely at the stamp. It was black and shiny, not matte like a tattoo would be. He rubbed at it with his thumb before replying.

What are you on about?

The numbers on the back of your hand. Scaring the hell out of me : (Got to get it off.

Ben stared for a second at the message, and then held his hand up to the light. She was right. Along the back of his hand, camouflaged by the swirls of the Futures logo, was a row of numbers. He twisted his hand round to try and read them. He squinted to make out the tiny printed digits. They read *22052014*.

He laid his hand flat on the table and shook his head in disbelief. It didn't make any sense. Why would a club stamp numbers on the back of its customer's hands? Was it for a promotion?

What do the numbers mean??? he tapped urgently.

I don't know but not waiting to find out. Got appointment booked tomorrow to burn them off.

Tomorrow?

Why the rush? he asked. The reply confused him further.

Only got a month left.

What the hell did that mean? A month until what?

What's happening in a month? He hit send and frowned at the screen as he waited for the reply.

The date on my hand is in one month. Don't know what's going to happen and don't want to. If I get it off in time I might avoid it. When is your date?

Ben held up his hand and looked carefully at the numbers. *22052014*. The 22nd of May, 2014. He shivered.

It couldn't be a promotion. If it had been, surely the club would have stamped the same date on every hand? Ben pulled out his phone and texted Tim. He was obviously at a loose end, because he replied quickly.

Yeah mate- well weird! Just noticed it. My numbers are 16042014- what's it for? So Tim had different numbers too- over a month earlier, if the date theory was correct. Ben pushed his phone aside and returned to the laptop.

Has anyone else got numbers?

Hundreds. Look here- After the message, she'd given a link to a website. Ben clicked it and scanned the homepage. He scrolled through page after page of messages from people, all over the country, all in the same situation. The circumstances followed a pattern: sexy girl or bloke invites you to secret club full of beautiful people, you get a sharp stamp on your hand, and then you wake up alone with a date that won't wash off. A date in the future… *Futures*. Something strange was going on.

He clicked on the link marked 'Theories', the stamp on his hand burning. The theories were outrageous, to say the least: ghosts, aliens, time-travellers, grim-reapers, angels, fairies and government spies- all were represented, discussed and ridiculed. No one had a clue. He scratched at the stamp, wincing as the raw skin stung painfully.

He toggled screens to return to the discussion page.

What happens on the date?

The page stared back at him as he waited for a reply. He hit refresh and leaned back in his chair. After five minutes, he typed again.

Why is it a date? What does it mean? What happens?

Ben hit 'send' and waited, tapping his fingers impatiently on the desk. He refreshed the page again after five minutes, and every five minutes after that. After an hour, he gave up. She obviously wasn't there anymore.

He switched off the laptop and went into the bathroom. His reflection in the mirror looked tired and old. Andy was right- he did look like death. He rubbed his hand over his face and caught sight of the stamp in the mirror. He scowled at the black ink on his hand but couldn't rouse the energy to try another futile attempt at removing it. Instead, he got into bed and burrowed under the covers.

Some people believe in fate, that things happen for a reason. Ben didn't really subscribe to the whole 'cosmic-

Karma-God-has-a-plan' idea, but he couldn't deny that the hated stamp changed his life.

The immediate effect was that he lost his job. It was ugly. Andy had been waiting for him the next day, with a company witness and a stern expression. He took one look at the shadows under Ben's eyes and the stubborn stamp and called him in to the office, told him to collect his things and phoned security to have him escorted from the premises. After a last-ditch attempt to save his job- not that he really wanted it- a pathetic display of pleading that fell on deaf ears, Ben finally lost the plot and told Andy to shove it. He marched out of the grim office, flanked by two shame-faced security guards, with his ex-colleagues' applause ringing in his ears. Even though he'd blown a steady job, he couldn't bring himself to care. He was free to do anything he wanted now. He just wished he knew what that was.

His future was taken care of, though. The next day, he'd bumped into an old school-mate, Jack, who owned a small but successful company specialising in sourcing and selling vintage vinyl. Over a pint in Ben's local, Jack offered him a job, travelling around the country to view and buy collections from sellers. Ben had almost bitten his hand off. This would be a complete change from spending his days slouched over a keyboard, clock-watching until the time when he was released from the torment an unfulfilling job brings. He couldn't believe his luck when he found out the position included a company car and an expenses account. They shook on the deal and ordered another pint to celebrate.

Time passed and life had turned out even better than Ben had ever hoped for. He had money, freedom, and an awesome boss who- far from wanting to curb Ben's social life- actively encouraged it. Ben was invited to glitzy parties at the coolest clubs, all in the name of promotion.

The stamp had been a lucky charm, forcing him to change his life. He looked at it now with affection, still clear and as fresh as it had looked that night, all those months ago. His star was on the rise and somehow that it was all due to those tiny black numbers, whatever they meant. He never had heard back from that girl on the forum. Probably she hadn't needed to post anymore once she'd had her stamp lasered off. He didn't think much about the date theory; the numbers probably didn't mean anything. May was months in the future, anyway.

The seasons changed. The daylight hours lasted longer and the post-Christmas spending slump started to lift. Business picked up and Ben was busier than ever. He still met up with Tim, though not so often now as he travelled so much. They caught up in Ben's local about once a month. Tim hadn't changed: still stuck in a dead-end job, still drinking in seedy clubs, still single. Ben suspected Tim was a bit jealous of his success. He urged him to quit and come and work for Jack.

"Seriously, it's a doddle. You just turn up in your flash car, sneer at their collection like you're doing them a favour, wave a bit of cash and watch them jump at the chance to sell it to you cheap. You can't go wrong. Jack will take anything. He says that the weirder it is, the rarer it is, and that means that someone, somewhere, will pay bucket-loads of cash for it. It's just a waiting game. The money's great, the perks are unbelievable and you'd have your pick of the birds!"

Tim took a swig of his pint before replying.

"I dunno, mate," he began. "It sounds a bit like hard work. All that driving around and networking and stuff? You know me, I'm can't be bothered with all that- I'd be terrible. At least at my place I get left alone if I keep my head down."

He took another sip before continuing. "Thanks and everything, but I'll sort myself out." He leaned back and shoved his fists into his pockets defiantly, staring at the floor to avoid Ben's disapproving look.

Ben sighed and shook his head in despair at Tim's attitude. He just didn't understand him sometimes. He seemed perfectly content to sit around and wait for something to happen to him, like fate was going to mysteriously intervene and change his life for him. He reached for his pint and uttered what was meant to be a withering put-down.

"I suppose you'll just be stuck at that rubbish job until your numbers come up, then." Tim looked up at him sharply. A slow grin spread over his face. He pulled his hand out of his jacket pocket and held it in front of him, palm facing away. The green ink shimmered as he flexed his fingers and gazed at it with a thoughtful expression.

"Numbers…yeah." His grin widened until it split his face. "I'll win the Lottery and then I won't have to work at all! These numbers have got to mean something, right? What if they're my winning numbers?" He peered closer. "It could be 1, 6, 42, 13… or 16, 21… whatever. I'll just keep trying 'til I get it." Satisfied that his problems were solved, he drained his pint and smacked his lips. Ben was incredulous.

"So that's it? Some hot girl stamps the winning lottery numbers on your hand and fixes your life? Who do you think she was- Mystic Meg?"

Tim shrugged, unconcerned by his friend's scorn.

"Well, why not? It's no less likely than seeing them in a dream, like that girl that won last year reckoned she did. I'm going to give it a try. Another pint?" He waved his glass under Ben's nose but Ben had had enough- both of beer and his friend's stupid ideas.

"No, thanks. I've got to get off." He stood up and pulled on his coat.

"Suit yourself." Tim waved a dismissive goodbye as he headed for the bar, intent on spending his anticipated winnings.

Ben frowned as he waited for a taxi. Why did he even bother with Tim anymore? Old habits, he guessed. They'd been mates and drinking buddies for so long that he hadn't seen how different they'd become until now. Without the shared experience of hating their jobs and getting wasted every weekend, the cracks had begun to show. He was no tabloid psychic but he predicted it would be a while before he rang Tim again. Lottery numbers… what a ridiculous idea. His taxi pulled up and Ben climbed in the back, rubbing his stamp thoughtfully as he was driven home through the rain-soaked streets.

He was too busy to call Tim over the next couple of months, and Tim didn't seem too worried about calling him either. Even though it was what Ben had expected, and even wanted, the death of their friendship stung. He buried himself in work, burning the candle at both ends and living life to the full, trying to fill the increasing emptiness inside him with alcohol and one-night-stands. He knew he was becoming a cliché. He drove the length and breadth of Britain to secure deals, and spent his nights in a succession of glamorous clubs and swanky parties, with a different girl on his arm every time. His commissions grew larger, and his car was upgraded.

Jack was delighted with him and said he was the best dealer the company had ever had. There was talk of sending him abroad- all expenses paid, naturally- to make deals with the larger recording companies that had taken an interest in remastering and rereleasing some of their rarer finds. Ben revelled in his success, but couldn't shake the stubborn sadness that he had no-one to share it with. An empty space grew inside him that he couldn't fill with alcohol and easy women. He was getting tired of one-night-stands and brief flings; he wanted something more, something meaningful.

He started thinking about Cassie again. It had only been one night, but she was different- special. He found that he was comparing the beautiful women that threw themselves at him with her, and finding them not up to her standard. They didn't have her perfect mouth, or delectable smell. He couldn't imagine spending every day with any of them- not like he had with Cassie. With someone like Cassie, he could have a future, be happy, and be whole. He wondered how he might find her. He had more to offer her now- this time she might stay.

He searched the internet for models named Cassie or Cassandra but, as lovely as the images were, none of them was the girl he was looking for. He went back to the place where he thought the club had been, time and time again, but he could not find it. It was as if it had never existed. He became obsessed with the idea of seeing her again, and imagined her honey-golden eyes smiling up at him as she wrapped her arms around his neck. He looked for her everywhere, his eyes scanning crowds in the hope of spotting her perfect features amongst the faces. She remained elusive. The only proof of her was stamped on his hand. The black ink was a constant reminder of that night, his only link to her.

He even went back to the website he had found while looking for ways to remove the stamp, but it offered no leads; the dwindling posts did, however, throw up something unexpected. Something was happening with the numbers, and it was happening to a lot of people.

He read post after post talking about the numbers- and

their meaning. They *were* dates. One post from a woman saying her boyfriend had proposed unexpectedly on the date stamped on her hand. Another, who had won a promotion. Still more, with photos to prove their claims, linking the date stamps with significant and life-changing events. A baby, four days early- a record deal- a publishing contract- the list went on.

Ben read the stories and peered at the blurry images taken with mobile phones and his heart lifted. He'd known all along there was something special about the numbers. Now he had proof. They *were* lucky. He'd had nothing but good fortune since he was stamped- was it possible that his date would bring something even better? He pulled back his long sleeve and read them again, although he knew them by heart after months of seeing them.

22052014. The 22nd of May, 2014. It was April. Just over a month to go. He stroked the black ink as he considered the possibilities. Promotion? Possible. Baby? Unlikely- or at least he hoped so; he wasn't aware of fathering any children eight months ago. A proposal? No- he froze as an image of Cassie's laughing face flashed across his mind. She was the only woman he could imagine spending the rest of his life with. Could it be..? Could it be the date he would meet Cassie again? A warm glow spread across him as he contemplated the idea. It would be almost too perfect- poetic even. A significant and life-changing event.

He glanced over at the calendar on the wall. It was the thirteenth of April. Three days before Tim's date. He had to tell him. A quick look at the clock on the wall told him it was nearly midnight but he grabbed his phone and pressed the speed-dial option anyway. He hadn't spoken to Tim in months but he couldn't let him miss out on this.

Tim answered, sounding sleepy.

"Hello?"

Ben took a deep breath.

"Tim? Mate, it's Ben. Listen, I've got something to tell you that will blow your mind! You know those numbers on the stamp? They're for real! It's on the internet and everything. There's hundreds of people with them." He paused to let this information sink in. "Mate, are you there?"

"Yeah, yeah, I'm here. What do you mean, they're real?"

"There are people on the internet posting about the numbers and how they've brought them good luck. You have to buy a lottery ticket- I'm serious! You're going to win!" Ben realised he had raised his voice.

Tim grunted.

"Nah, mate. I've already tried it. I spent a month buying tickets for every lottery I could find. I used every combination of numbers I could make from the ones on my hand- waste of time. And now I'm skint."

Ben paced the floor as he spoke, too keyed up to sit.

"The numbers aren't the secret- the date they make is! The sixteenth of April 2014- the night of the draw. You could buy a lucky dip and still win; it doesn't matter which numbers you pick. You have to try it at least. I'll lend you a couple of quid if you need it."

Tim sounded a bit more awake now.

"I'm not *that* skint, mate. I can afford a lottery ticket. Where's all this come from? You laughed at me when I said it ages ago."

"I know, and I'm sorry. I didn't realise it until tonight." Ben reached for his laptop and clicked on one of the pictures as he spoke. "It's all here. There are pictures of the stamps and then people saying what happened to them on that date. I'll give you the website." He reeled off the address and waited while Tim, wide awake now, turned on his laptop.

While he listened to him grunting and shuffling to find the plug to charge it, Ben smiled at how easy it was, talking to Tim again. He realised he'd missed him.

"Right, got it." Ben waited while Tim clicked his way through the pages, chuckling and letting out little whoops as he found story after story of good fortune. "Whoa... *This* is what the numbers are for?" Ben could hear the smile in his voice. "This is mental! I am definitely buying a ticket!"

"I told you! *'Significant and life-changing event'-* that's what they all say. You can't get much more life-changing than winning the lottery!"

"Nah, mate. I think you'll find *I* told *you*!" Tim laughed, with no trace of hard feelings over their falling-out. "Life-changing... Cheers, mate- seriously."

"Hey, no problem. That's what mates are for, right?"

"Right," Tim agreed. "Pub, Wednesday, to celebrate? I want a big crowd when my numbers come up!" Ben laughed and agreed. They made plans to meet on Wednesday night and Ben hung up the phone. He doubted Tim would sleep until then. Right now, he was too wired to sleep himself.

If Tim won on Wednesday, it would prove that the numbers had a purpose, that they had some sort of magical power to predict or induce massive life-changing events. The stories on the website were convincing but Ben knew he'd need to see it with his own eyes to really believe it. He couldn't allow himself to hope until then. He squashed down the bubble of excitement. He knew his date had something to do with Cassie. He undressed, climbed into bed and eventually fell asleep, dreaming of her smile.

All day Wednesday, Ben was on edge. Tonight's result meant more to him than Tim becoming a millionaire, as awesome as that would be. He hardly dared think it consciously, but a small flame of hope was burning inside him, threatening to engulf given the slightest encouragement. Hope that seeing Cassie again was a possibility or, given the stamps' remarkable track-record so far, a certainty.

For the first time ever in his new job, he clock-watched. He was in the main office today, going over some paperwork with Jack for the international deal. His boss was going on holiday in a couple of weeks and he wanted everything to be ready before he left. Ben couldn't stop his leg from bouncing up and down under the table, or stop his eyes flicking towards his watch every few minutes. Jack noticed his distracted mood and asked him, pointedly, if he was looking forward to going to China.

"What? Oh- yeah, yeah. Can't wait." Ben's smile was tight with anticipation of that night but he tried to make it look genuine for Jack. He didn't want Jack to think he wasn't committed to finishing the deal. They'd both worked hard on it and it was going to make them both a lot of money.

Not as much as Tim's going to win tonight...

Ben's leg started bouncing again and Jack glanced at him curiously. He silenced the errant thought and managed to get through the rest of the meeting giving his full attention to what Jack was saying.

When they'd finished the meeting, Jack handed Ben an envelope.

"Here are your tickets, and the flight and hotel details. A car will collect you and there'll be another waiting when you land in Beijing. Don't lose these between now and next month." Ben opened the envelope and peeked inside at his tickets to China. His eyes caught the date and a hot tingle ran over his body.

Departure date: 22/05/2014

This was it. It was happening. He was flying to Beijing on

the date stamped onto his hand. This couldn't be a coincidence. He thanked Jack and wished him a relaxing holiday before turning and almost running for the lift. When the doors shut and no one was watching, he punched the air in glee and let out a hiss of delight. This would be the day he'd find Cassie, he just knew it!

That night, Ben bounced into the pub, buoyant with anticipation. He looked around for Tim, and found him sat at a corner table near the widescreen TV. He looked green and clammy with nerves. Ben ordered a pint and joined him, sliding round the bench until their knees were almost touching.

"Alright?" he asked. Tim grimaced.

"I feel sick, mate. It's a rollover- 13.4 million!" He gestured towards the ticket clutched in his hand, the one with the stamp. It twinkled and winked, Ben imagined. He whooped and slapped Tim on the back.

"Mate, that's amazing! What are you going to spend it on?"

Tim gulped his drink before answering.

"I haven't got it yet, have I?" He didn't look like a man who was thrilled with the prospect of becoming a millionaire. In fact, he looked like a man about to be executed. His eyes were rimmed with dark circles, and he chewed on the fingernails of his free hand nervously. Ben took the ticket from his sweaty grasp and read the numbers.

"Lucky dip? Good choice. It's going to happen anyway- why complicate it by choosing the wrong numbers?" His attempt at mood-lightening humour went down like a lead balloon. "What's the time? How long have you got left being poor?" He handed back the ticket. Tim put it in his breast pocket and patted it to reassure himself it was in there.

"Ten minutes. What if we're wrong, though?" he groaned miserably. "It's crazy- how could some random numbers from a stupid tattoo-stamp mean I'm going to win the lottery?" He patted his pocket again, though. "What if it means something completely different? Or doesn't mean anything at all?"

His eyes pleaded silently for reassurance. Ben was bound by the laws of man-friendship, so could only offer support by punching Tim in the arm. Tim swayed to the side slightly and took another drink.

"This is it, mate. I know it," said Ben. "This is what you want. This is your significant and life-changing event, happening right now. You should be enjoying it!" Ben didn't add that his own hopes were pinned on tonight's outcome too. He wasn't quite ready to admit out loud that the significant and life-changing event he wished for the most was a near-stranger named Cassie. This *was* Tim, after all.

He called over to the barman.

"Hey, mate- can you stick the TV on? My friend wants to check his lottery numbers." The barman obliged; Wednesdays were always quiet and he quite fancied checking his numbers too. He bought a ticket every week, regular as clockwork, and dreamed of a little bar in Spain.

The two men waited anxiously as the minutes ticked by. The pub hummed as people chatted and drank. Tim vibrated with nervous energy. Ben's leg started to bounce as the time for the draw approached. Neither man spoke. Tim patted his pocket. Finally the screen lit up with the jazzy opening credits of the lottery draw.

Tim sat up ramrod-straight and stared at the screen, the whites of his eyes showing. Ben's eyes flicked back and forth between the TV and his friend; Tim had a sheen of perspiration on his top lip and looked like he might faint in a very unmanly way.

The presenter finished speaking and invited the guest, some bloke from a talent show that Ben only vaguely recognised, to push the big button. Tim made a gurgling sound and stopped breathing, his eyes still locked on the screen. Ben punched his arm again until he inhaled. He wondered if anyone had ever had a heart-attack from seeing their numbers come up. He glanced quickly around the pub; no one was paying any attention to them.

The coloured balls whirled around the glass sphere, hovering playfully. Ben couldn't bear it. His leg bounced until it jolted the table. Tim had one hand on his heart, held over the pocket where the winning ticket lay. He looked like he was about to stand up and sing the national anthem. Ben snorted, almost hysterical with tension. Tim didn't move an inch. The first ball dropped into the chute and rolled lazily into the tray.

A number flashed up on the screen. A six. Ben looked quickly at Tim for his reaction. He'd turned a funny shade of fuchsia. Ben missed the second ball as it settled into place next to the first. He knew it was the right one, though, as Tim's eyes had opened wider than he thought was possible. Fifteen. This was real. The next twenty seconds seemed to pass in a heartbeat, until all six balls were lined up neatly in the tray. There was a moment of silence as it sank in.

Suddenly, Tim let out a huge yell, his face purple. His hand curled into a fist as he clutched the ticket through the material of his pocket. He took a deep breath and turned to Ben, grinning at him despite tearful eyes.

"I've *won*!" he whispered in awe. Ben stuck out his own hand to congratulate him, but Tim pushed it away, standing up quickly, overturning the low table and knocking their glasses to the floor. He began to jump up and down, whooping and yelling. Ben jumped up to join him and they bounced together, hugging and laughing, as the bemused onlookers watched. Eventually, Tim stopped to catch his breath. He held Ben at arm's length and beamed at him. Ben's smile, for different reasons, matched his friend's.

"I've won!" Tim shouted again, before rushing to the bar and ordering a round of drinks for everyone, including the barman who, fittingly, poured himself a small bitter. He was soon surrounded by a crowd of well-wishers and new friends, eager to slap his back and get his phone number.

Ben let Tim revel in his new-found popularity and sat back down, righting the table and sweeping up the glass with his foot. He had reason to celebrate too, but more privately. Tonight was proof, if more proof were needed, of the numbers' power. They made things happen. Looking over at Tim's ecstatic expression, Ben had no doubt that his friend's dearest wish had been granted tonight.

Ben knew what his dearest wish was. Just as the stamp had remained stubbornly visible on his skin for all these months, Cassie's name had been tattooed invisibly on his heart. She was the one; he'd never met anybody like her and, soon, he would see her again. They had a date. He grinned gleefully, a secret smile, and prepared to reclaim his friend from the throng. They had a long night of celebrating to enjoy.

The next few weeks were hectic, even as they were slow. Despite the mammoth and constant task of juggling his job with baby-sitting Tim as he attempted to do a "Brewster's Millions", the days still crawled by for Ben as he counted down to his date. Tim kept him physically busy; when he wasn't dragging him to view cars or ridiculously-large yachts, he was badgering him to choose his "thank you" present.

Tim desperately wanted to spend some of his millions on a gift for his friend, but there was only one thing that Ben wanted, and money couldn't buy her.

He felt like a kid again, impatiently waiting for Christmas to arrive. He mentally ticked off the days until his flight to Beijing and packed, then re-packed, his case at least ten times. His enthusiasm whenever his trip was discussed at work was real, but not for the reasons Jack imagined. Ben knew he would still do his best to pull the deal off successfully of course, but the thrill of anticipation was less about finalising the contract and more- all- about reuniting with Cassie.

The more he obsessed about it, the more convinced he became that she was the one. He was twenty-eight now, and tired of playing the field. He realised, with a little surprise, that what he wanted now was a proper relationship with someone he could spend the rest of his life with. Even though it had been brief, his night with Cassie had been the only time he'd ever felt that he'd found that someone special. He couldn't rationalise it; he just knew it to be true.

The weekend before his date, Ben was at home. He was packing- again- and Tim had come round with his new laptop to ask Ben how it worked. He'd parked himself on the bedroom floor so he could talk to Ben while he rearranged his suitcase. As Ben watched Tim play with his latest toy, he was struck by how false the saying "money can't buy you happiness" was. He'd never seen Tim so happy. He'd quit his boring job, sent his mum on a cruise, splashed out on a new car, and was in the process of purchasing a swanky house with twenty acres of land. What he'd do with all that land, Ben didn't know. But Tim wanted it, so Tim pulled out his new platinum card and bought it.

He was both impetuous and generous. His new trick was

to gift money to unsuspecting members of the public. Last week, he'd dropped two hundred quid into a busker's case because he liked the song he was playing, quickly walking away and hiding round the corner to watch, giggling like a school-boy, as the musician stopped and bent down to pick it up. He told Ben that seeing their faces was the best part- it made him feel like he'd brightened up their day. Ben had to remind him that he'd have nothing left for himself if didn't rein it in a little. Tim scoffed.

"The amount of interest I'm earning in ten minutes is more than most people's yearly salary," he argued. "I can afford to spread a little love- it's not like I earned it!" Ben couldn't think of anything to say to that.

Right now, Tim wasn't looking like he wanted to spread the love; he looked like he wanted to hurl his new laptop across the room.

"Why do they make it so damn difficult?" he grumbled. "And why are all the instructions in Japanese?" He thrust the manual, a flimsy excuse for guidance printed on a single sheet of A4 paper, at Ben. "Come on, mate. Help me out here!"

Ben glanced briefly at the tiny writing and passed the sheet back with a grin.

"It's Chinese," he said, turning back to his case. "And you need to press the green button on the front." Tim goggled at him before holding the paper, upside down, and peering at the characters.

"Whoa… I didn't know you could read Chinese! Did you have to learn it for your deal?"

Ben laughed.

"I can't, you moron. It says on the box that the instructions are also in Chinese, and the button-" He reached over and pressed the green button, "-has POWER written next to it." He chuckled as the machine whirred quietly to life. "All this money and still no brains…"

Tim screwed the manual into a small ball and threw it at Ben.

"Alright, show-off."

He waited the seconds that it took the laptop to boot up, and clicked on the internet connection icon. Ben folded his best suit trousers carefully and laid them on top of the matching jacket. He wanted to look smart and professional for his meeting, but they'd also come in handy when he took Cassie out for dinner. His stomach clenched at his unconscious use of the word "when" in his thoughts.

"Yeah- now we're cooking!" Tim squealed as he typed in the address bar. Ben put down the shoes that he was holding- they needed another polish before they went back in the case- and sat down next to Tim.

"What you looking for?" He knew the kind of websites Tim usually visited.

"That website about the stamps," Tim replied. "I'm going to put my picture up and tell everyone how rich I am."

"I thought you'd have done that already."

"Not had time. It's been a busy few weeks and then I couldn't work out how to take a picture on my new phone, or get this laptop to work." He clicked to upload his picture. "But you sorted that out so now I'm ready to share my good news."

Ben watched as Tim typed a caption to go with the photo. He should put his own stamp on, really. He only had a few days before his date and he was hoping to be occupied for quite a while after… He smiled his secret smile. He still hadn't shared his theory with Tim. Every time Tim had asked him what he hoped his significant and life-changing event would be, Ben had pretended not to have any ideas. He told Tim he was looking forward to being surprised.

He stood up and returned to his case to hide his smirk. Tim finished with his picture and began scrolling through the gallery of photos and captions. There were quite a few now; Ben knew because he checked regularly, every tale of good fortune added to his conviction that, in five short days, he would find Cassie. Maybe she'd be at the airport, or even on the plane. Perhaps they'd end up sat next to each other: that would be perfect. He'd have all those hours to charm her and let her see how they were meant to be together.

He hummed happily as he folded and refolded, responding occasionally to Tim's comments or questions as he looked at the gallery. Tim kept up a constant inane chatter that Ben could easily keep track of as his mind wandered elsewhere. He walked over to his wardrobe to look at his selection of ties.

"Hang on-" Tim fell silent for the first time in twenty minutes.

"What?" Ben asked, not turning round.

"Yours is black, yeah?"

"Eh?"

"Your stamp. The stamps in the pictures are green. Mine is green. Yours is black. There aren't any pictures of stamps with black ink." Tim held up his hand as evidence. The ink was fading: it had started to fade after his win, but there was no mistaking its colour. Ben walked over and pulled the laptop towards him.

"Yeah, there is. I've seen them." He clicked on a few pictures until he found one. He pushed the laptop back to Tim and pointed at a picture. The stamp showed clearly, in black ink, a date from the last week. Ben read the caption under it, posted a few days before that.

Not long to go now!!! Can't wait for my turn! :)

There wasn't a follow-up message. Tim peered at the

picture and frowned.

"He's not said what happened to him on the date."

Ben shrugged, unconcerned, and continued packing.

"Maybe he's in the Bahamas. Too busy drinking cocktails and sunbathing to share his story." He held up two shirts, trying to decide which one Cassie would fancy him in the most. Tim shook his head as if trying to shake his thoughts into a meaningful order.

"They have the internet in the Bahamas, surely? Why would he bother posting his picture and then not follow it up?" Tim clicked through a few more pictures. "Look. Another black stamp- dated February. No comment about what happened there, either." He held up the laptop for Ben to see.

"It doesn't mean anything," Ben said. "I bet there's loads of stamps where people haven't come back to say what happened." Despite his words, an uneasy shiver ran down Ben's spine. What if only the green ones worked? Maybe the others hadn't posted a significant and life-changing event because they hadn't experienced one? He rubbed his stamp, anxiously. He couldn't bear it if his didn't follow through on its promise. It wouldn't be fair. Tim had what he wanted- why couldn't Ben have Cassie?

"Yeah, but-"

"Just leave it, ok?" Ben snapped. He immediately regretted it. He wasn't angry with Tim, but this discovery had him rattled. He realised how much he needed something to happen to him on his date, how much he was expecting. The possibility that the date would come and go with no significance was beyond disappointing. It was disastrous.

He turned to Tim with an apologetic smile.

"Sorry, mate. I guess I'm just a bit tired and stressed out about this deal. Jack's relying on me for it to go smoothly and

I don't want to let him down."

Tim shrugged and stood up, closing the laptop and tucking it under his arm.

"No worries. I should be getting off anyway- got stuff to do."

"More cars to buy?" Ben teased. Tim laughed.

"Yeah, I've been thinking about getting one of those classic cars- something a bit retro and cool. Might impress the girls." Despite his new admirers, Tim was still single. He was proving surprisingly fussy considering his previous low standards. "I'll see you before you go, yeah?"

"Course. Meet up for a drink in the week?"

"I'm free any day- jobless, you know?" They both chuckled.

Ben saw Tim out and shut the door. He leaned against it, his forehead resting on the hard wood. He chewed his bottom lip anxiously as he fought the urge to switch on his laptop and look more closely at the black stamps. It must just be coincidence that Tim had found those two. Ben knew, if he looked, that he'd find stamps like his with accompanying posts of life-changing events. Searching for them would feel like questioning their power, though, and a new superstitious part of him vowed not to look for that reason. He didn't want to jinx himself. He had to believe that his stamp meant something- that something important would happen to him on that date. Maybe the power came from belief?

He straightened up and returned to his packing, working hard to believe as he folded and refolded, selected and rejected. His stamp would work. His date would come. After a while, he began to hum happily.

The morning of the 22nd of May, 2014, Ben woke before his alarm went off. He sprang out of bed with a grin on his

STAMP

face and sang while he was in the shower, caressing his stamp gently as he washed, not wanting it to rub off now. He whistled as he made his breakfast and polished his shoes one last time. He changed his outfit twice and spent ten minutes on his hair before he was satisfied with his appearance. He wheeled his case to the front door and looked at his watch. He was ready ridiculously early. He flicked on the TV while he waited and watched the breakfast news, his fingertips drumming on the arm of the leather sofa.

What would he say to Cassie when he saw her? He'd have to be cool, casual, not needy- a girl like Cassie would run a mile if he appeared desperate. He wondered where he'd see her. Would she be at the airport? He patted his pocket to check he had his clip of business cards. They were there in his inside pocket: ready to give to her if it was only a brief encounter in the terminal or lounge. He also had a pen so he could take her number too. He'd thought of everything.

He really hoped she'd be on the plane. For days, he'd been rehearsing their conversation in his head. He imagined her delight at bumping in to him. *What are the chances?* she'd say, smiling up at him with her perfect lips. He'd act surprised too; he wouldn't tell her that he'd known for weeks that they were going to meet today. The flight to Beijing was long: they'd have hours to talk. In fact, he was sure they'd have the rest of their lives. Once he found her again, he wasn't going to let her go.

He checked his watch again. Almost time to leave. He turned off the TV and watched out of the window until his taxi pulled up outside. He smoothed his hair one last time before grabbing his case and leaving, taking a final look around his flat before closing and locking the door. He hurried down the steps and into the waiting car.

The traffic was unusually quiet for that hour in the morning and Ben arrived at the airport in plenty of time. He paid the driver and wheeled his case towards the checking-in desk. He joined the queue for his flight and scanned the crowded area, fighting the urge to hop impatiently from one foot to the other. No sign of her yet.

The queue shuffled forward slightly and he nudged his case forward with his perfectly-polished shoe. The case was heavy, full of extra clothes to cover every possible romantic situation from beach to bar to bedroom. He turned to look around for her again. He wondered if she had already checked in. He looked at the time on the board; he wasn't late, but maybe she'd arrived early to beat the crowds and do a bit of shopping in duty-free. His shoulders relaxed; she was probably already sipping a coffee in the departures lounge. He nudged his case forward again, willing the people in front to move more quickly so he could join her there.

The queue crept forward steadily and he dutifully filled each gap that opened up before him. It wasn't much longer before he reached the check-in desk. The woman behind the desk had perfect hair but too much make-up. She smiled brightly as he loaded his case onto the scales, revealing startlingly white teeth.

"Good morning, sir. May I see your ticket and passport, please?"

Ben tore his eyes away from the impressive veneers and handed over his documents, fidgeting while she tapped on her keyboard and attached a label to the handle of his case.

"Would you be interested in upgrading to first-class today, sir?" she asked, eyeing his smart suit. Ben considered this for a moment. He'd never travelled in first class before; he didn't even know how much it cost.

"No, thank you," he replied finally. "Not today."

"No problem."

She handed him his boarding card, which he tucked into the inside pocket of his suit jacket.

"Enjoy your flight." Again the dazzling smile.

"Thank you."

Ben checked the time on his phone as he walked towards the security control. He had a couple of hours before he departed. He also had a message from Tim, wishing him good luck and asking whether his event had happened yet. He didn't reply; it was still early in the day. He pushed his phone back into his pocket and joined the queue.

He tried to look casual as his eyes searched the faces of the travellers lined up in front of the row of metal-detectors and scanners. His heart skipped a beat every time a petite figure with long, ebony hair caught his eye. But it was never her.

"Move along, please."

A burly security guard waved him forward. He reminded Ben of Levi, the bouncer from the club. They had the same impressive bulk and penetrating gaze. Ben emptied the contents of his pockets into a tray, removed his jacket and shoes, and walked through the metal-detector. He smiled at his own relief that it stayed silent. Those things always made him nervous. He re-joined the line and waited for his tray to pop out of the scanner.

The man in front of him reached for his own tray and, as his hand stretched and his sleeve pulled back slightly, Ben spotted something black and familiar, the swirls and digits partially covered by the thick, blond hair that tufted out from his wrist. Before he had a chance to react, the man had scooped his belongings out of the tray and into his pockets and hurried off to the departure lounge.

Ben opened his mouth to call out to him, but a nudge in

his back took his attention. He muttered an apology to the peeved-looking woman behind him and emptied his tray. When he looked up again, the man had gone.

Ben's heartbeat quickened; he was sure that man had a black stamp. He hadn't had a good look at the digits, but the design was unmistakeable. Apart from Tim, he'd never seen any others in real life, only photos on a website. He wondered if the man was on the website too. He rubbed his own stamp with the fingers of his other hand. It was a strange coincidence to see one here today. He wondered what it meant, or even if it meant anything at all. He pushed gently through the crowds of people milling around the entrance to the departure lounge and made his way inside.

The lounge was quieter than he expected, perhaps because it was a Thursday. He'd only travelled at weekends before: lads' holidays or the occasional romantic break. Thinking of romance brought his mind back to Cassie. He rubbed his stamp again for luck and began searching the shops and bars.

In the newsagents, he bought a newspaper and some mints. As he handed over the cash, he noticed the woman behind the till stare at his hand. He waited until she lifted her eyes to his face and then raised his eyebrows questioningly. She blushed.

"Sorry, I was just wondering what they were for. Is it a convention or something?"

"I beg your pardon?"

"The thing on your hand. It's just that there's quite a lot of you today. I wondered if it was because you were meeting up or something." She flushed an even brighter shade of pink at his expression. Ben realised he was frowning and made an effort to soften his features. He smiled and made his tone pleasant.

"Really? You've seen more of these today?"

"Yeah. It's a bit unusual. Most of the time, they give people those cards to hang around their necks, or name badges. I've not seen ones like that before."

"Yes, it is unusual." Ben went along with her assumption and didn't offer any further explanation- not that he could have given her one if he'd wanted to. So there were more people with stamps here today? That was intriguing.

"Where did the others go?" he asked casually.

The woman shrugged her shoulders and shook her head.

"I'm sorry, I don't know."

"Ok. Thank you." Ben smiled again, took his shopping and left.

He made his way to a nearby bar. As he ordered a coffee, he sneaked a look at the hands of the other customers waiting to be served. No stamps. He raised his head and scanned the room casually. No Cassie either. He took his drink and chose a corner table where he had a good view of the bar itself and the avenue outside. He sipped his coffee and watched the people walking past. None of them were Cassie. He only had a short time left before he boarded the plane. Surely he would see her soon? The balloon of excitement that had been slowly growing inside him over the last few weeks began to deflate. He'd been so sure that she'd be here today.

He stared down at his stamp; it seemed to burn coldly. Stupid thing. Stupid him- thinking they had a date. It wasn't special at all. There were probably hundreds of people with stupid stamps in this lounge, and Ben was willing to bet that none of them were mooning over missed opportunities and life-changing events that wouldn't happen. Maybe Tim was right; maybe the black stamps were duds. Ben sighed. As much as he was trying to snap himself out of it, that tiny flame of hope still burned. Maybe she was running late; maybe she was just arriving now. He knew he wouldn't give up yet.

The minutes passed and his coffee cooled as he waited and watched. To distract himself from his nerves, he walked around the shops again. He told himself he was just stretching his legs but he knew, deep down, that he was really still looking for her. He ordered another coffee and resumed his position in the bar. He checked the time: just under an hour before take-off. They'd be putting out the call for boarding soon. He drained his cup and stood. Might as well head that way; he could check the shops again as he walked.

Ben's head swivelled left and right as he strolled with forced casualness down the avenue towards his gate. He let his eyes roam over the faces of the shoppers, looked into every shop doorway and window. He paused to contemplate a display of scarves, smiling politely as an expensive-smelling blonde bumped past him. He followed her with his eyes, wondering what gave the rich the right to shove plebs, feeling butterflies begin to dance in his stomach as she swept through a door bearing a sign he hadn't noticed before.

First Class Lounge- of course!

Why hadn't he thought of that before? Cassie was sophisticated; she'd surely be travelling by first class. Ben cursed himself for not taking the opportunity to upgrade his seat. He wondered if he'd be able to sweet-talk one of the cabin crew into letting him switch seats once they were in the air.

He quickened his pace and headed towards the gate where he would board. He wanted to be there first so he could see when Cassie arrived, maybe talk to her before they got on the plane. He hurried to a jog, weaving in and out of the passengers who milled around, calling an apology over his shoulder to those he bumped.

When he reached his gate, puffing slightly, he was relieved

to see that they had only just started allowing the passengers to board. He scanned the crowd quickly but she wasn't there. He lingered at the back of the queue, letting other people go in front. He focussed his gaze on the faces as they passed him, searching for one in particular, trying to keep his own features composed. It was hard to keep track and twice Ben had to push in front in order to make sure he had not missed her. The flow of passengers increased, then dwindled until Ben realised that he was the last one left. He turned to look out of the door and down the corridor.

"Are you boarding this flight, sir?"

Ben turned back to face the uniformed, clean-shaven man who was addressing him in a tone that Tim would have called 'snotty'. His teeth were also unbelievably white. Ben wondered if it were a requirement of the job.

"Sir? Are you departing today? May I see your boarding pass?"

The man held out his hand, the other poised to summon security, should it be found that he was an intruder. His pose, faintly ridiculous, gave away the pleasure he took in his little bit of power. *Another jobs-worth.* Ben stifled a giggle, blinked, and forced a friendly smile onto his face.

"Yes, of course. Here."

He handed over his pass, which was duly inspected and handed back with a sniff. The man seemed almost disappointed that everything was in order.

"We will be closing the gates in five minutes, sir. If you are departing, you need to board now."

"Thank you. I was just-"

He broke off mid-sentence, eyes fixed on the man's hand as he held out the papers. It was a different colour to the rest of his skin, like badly-applied foundation. One part had smeared to reveal a black design underneath. A design that

Ben recognised. He reached out and grabbed the man's hand.

"Wait! Is that..?"

The man snatched his hand back guiltily, though he still managed to paste an offended look onto his face. He tucked his hand behind his back and drew himself up to his full height.

"Sir. If you wish to board the plane, please do so now. Otherwise, we shall call security and have you removed." He turned on his heel and marched away, holding his stamped hand close to his body.

Ben stared after him. Another stamp? Why? He could understand why he was trying to cover it up- the airline would be even stricter than Andy, his old boss, had been- but why were they so many of them here today? What did it have to do with Cassie? Was he on the same flight? He wanted to ask the man about his stamp but, before he had a chance, the man checked his watch and mouthed something to his colleague, before walking purposefully towards the gate.

"Wait!"

Ben jogged to the gate, holding out his boarding pass. The man paused and held the door open.

"Thank you, sir," he said, declining to inspect the document again. "Please board now."

"Are you flying today?" Ben asked. The man shook his head quickly.

"No. I changed my shift. I've got... something I need to do today." He licked his lips nervously. He was lying. Why was he lying about needing to change his shift?

Ben walked through the door, stopped, turned, and asked the question that was burning his tongue.

"When is your date?"

The man hesitated. He glanced quickly at his colleague, who was eyeing them warily- no doubt ready to call security over his strange behaviour. Finally, he looked Ben in the eye and answered.

"It's today. So are all the others."

Ben's eyes widened in surprise. He opened his mouth to ask more, but was cut off with a curt 'Enjoy your flight' before he was ushered through the door, which locked behind him with decisive finality.

He trotted down the tunnel in a daze. What was going on? Why were there so many people here with stamps like his? The man he'd seen at security, the airline employee- they both had stamps like his. Even the ink was the same colour. And the woman in the shop had said there were others here today too. Did they all have the same date? And, if so, why?

Ben didn't think this was anything to do with Cassie anymore. He had just been kidding himself if he thought the stamp was going to deliver him a happy ending. Something bigger was happening here, something that linked dozens of people- maybe more- with a black-inked stamp. But what? Unease settled on Ben's shoulders as his footsteps echoed around the tunnel. If only he could figure out the connection…

The tunnel ended and Ben stepped into the body of the plane, showed his boarding pass and was directed to his aisle seat on the right-hand side. It was the only one left empty, so it was easy to spot. In the seat next to his, a wave of ebony hair was bent low over a magazine, the overhead light making it gleam like raven's wings. Ben's heart skipped a beat, only to sink in disappointment as the woman raised her head to glance up at him as he sat down. She wasn't Cassie.

The plane hummed gently with the susurration of educated voices, suit-clad businessmen and women, making the awkward social chit-chat that was required on long flights such as these. Ben fidgeted in his seat, adjusting his jacket as he smiled tightly at the raven-haired woman sat to his left. She was dressed more sensibly for the journey, in an upmarket interpretation of jogging bottoms and a luxuriously soft jumper. She had a friendly face. She stretched out her hand to his.

"Hi, I'm Anna."

Ben took her hand in his and shook it politely. Her skin was soft too.

"I'm Ben."

Anna smiled with a gentle glow that lit up her face. She really was attractive, even if she wasn't the woman he'd hoped to see. Despite the confusion and disappointment, maybe things were looking up after all.

"I thought we should get acquainted before one of us inevitably falls asleep and dribbles on the other's shoulder," she chuckled. "But, if you prefer, we could always ignore each other for the next goodness-knows-how-many hours instead?" She cocked her head, emphasising the question with a slight lift of her eyebrow.

"No, consider my shoulder all yours," Ben replied, matching her teasing tone. Anna's smile widened. Was she *flirting* with him? Ben palm tingled, and he realised he was still holding her hand. He grinned shyly and lowered his eyes, releasing her fingers. As he did, he saw the familiar black ink on her skin. His eyes shot back up to her face.

"You have a stamp?"

"Oh, this?" she blushed. "Long story- a stubborn reminder of a drunken night out." She forced a laugh and held up her hand for Ben to see. The line of numbers was clear. 22052014. Today's date.

A nauseous pressure built in Ben's stomach.

"Excuse me-" he muttered, ignoring her surprised expression as he rose from his seat and made his way to the cubicles at the back of the plane.

"Sir? Excuse me- sir?" A flight attendant followed him down the narrow aisle. "Can I help you? You need to take your seat."

Ben ignored him and continued. The passengers either side, curious and concerned, turned their heads to watch him as he passed. The man raised his voice slightly and quickened his pace to catch him up.

"Sir, are you unwell? The plane will be departing shortly. Passengers must be seated now. You-"

He broke off mid-sentence as Ben halted suddenly and turned to face him, his face white and shiny with moisture. The man stepped back instinctively. Ben rubbed his hand across his damp forehead, noticing how the attendant's eyes followed the movement. Ben swallowed and tried to regain his composure.

"I'm sorry," he said. "I just came over a bit strange for a moment."

The attendant smiled sympathetically.

"I understand. It happens all the time." He began to lead Ben back to his seat. Ben followed, unresisting, feeling like he was not in control of his own body. "As soon as we're in the air, I'll fetch you a glass of water- or maybe something stronger, to steady your nerves?"

Ben wasn't listening. As he stumbled back down the aisle, only one thing held his attention. In every row, to both sides, in at least one seat, a black-stamped hand. The alarmed faces of his fellow passengers blurred into the background as the stamps seemed to surround him. *So many.* He swayed and held onto the head-rest of the seat next to him. *All on the same plane.* His thoughts were woolly, thick and tangled. *Black stamps- there's something about the black stamps.* He reached his seat and allowed himself to be buckled in. Anna edged away and busied herself in her magazine, not meeting his eye. The safety demonstration began, but Ben could only stare at the ink on his hand. May 22nd, 2014. Today. Now. *All the black stamps.*

The engines started up, a vibration under his feet that shook his body and made his teeth chatter. With a small lurch, the plane began to move, taxiing towards the runway. The sweat gathered on his forehead and a droplet fell onto his hand, wetting the ink that now sizzled on his flesh. *What happens to the black stamps?* The safety demonstration ended and the flight attendant took his seat with his colleagues.

Fragments of thought jostled for attention, his subconscious desperately trying to tell him something vitally important.

Futures…

Stamp…

Date…

Significant and life-changing event…

Black stamps…

Ben massaged his clammy brow, trying to connect the pieces of information, to focus over the increasing roar of the engines. What happened to the people with black stamps? Why did they never return to post on the website? What happened to them on their date?

He lifted his head and looked around at the people on the plane. Most of them were in their twenties, like him, or thirties at the most. Had they all been to a secret club named Futures? Why were there so many stamps here today? On this plane? What did they all have in common? Pressure pinned him against his seat as the plane accelerated. *What significant and life-changing event was going to happen to all these people today?*

All at once, the pieces of the puzzle slotted together and he knew. Cold terror rushed around his body as if his blood had turned to ice. The plane surged forward with a final thrust as the plane lifted its nose into the air and began to climb. Ben fumbled with his seatbelt and tried to stand. He had to get off of this plane!

"Sir, please! Sit back down and fasten your seatbelt!" one of the flight attendants shouted.

Ben managed to release the catch and struggle to his feet.

"We have to stop the plane! We have to get off!" he screamed. "The plane is going to—"

A loud bang drowned out his last words. The plane shuddered and lurched sharply to the left. The passengers screamed. Ben tumbled into the lap of a middle-aged businessman, his face greyer than the suit he wore. Their eyes locked for one terrible moment, their fear mirrored in the other's face.

"I shouldn't have been on this plane," the man sobbed, clutching Ben's hand as the broken turbines exploded in the left engine. "I was supposed to fly last week, but it was cancelled." His face was a grimace of terror and confusion. "I shouldn't be on this plane…"

Ben's eyes dropped to where his hand was locked in to the man's grasp. He read the matching numbers and understood why there were no posts from those with black stamps. As the plane banked steeply, too low, too fast, too close to avoid ploughing into the airport departure gate building where they had stood only minutes ago, Ben understood. He squeezed the man's hand, but it was not a gesture of comfort, more of numb acceptance. This was it. This was their significant and life-changing event. The remaining engine screamed as the pilot struggled to control their descent; the plane shook as it dropped towards the ground, towards the man in the departure gate building who had switched his shifts to avoid flying today.

"Yes, you should," he whispered, not even loud enough for the man to hear him. "We all should." The stamps on their hands, identical, seemed to laugh and jeer over the wails and shrieks that surrounded them. Ben closed his eyes and gripped the stranger's hand as an image of Cassie's laughing face flashed into his mind, for the last time.

"We are all supposed to be on this plane today."

ROCK GOD

Mia yelped as Darren grabbed hold of her wrist and yanked her up the stone steps of the converted theatre, not letting go until the bustling street was behind them and they were through the doors. She barely had time to take a breath before she was plunged into a heaving rabble of strangers, the smell of cigarette smoke and stale beer besieging her nose like a smog of fast-living and reckless attitudes.

"Come on," he called over his shoulder. "We don't want to be late."

"I'm coming," she said, rubbing her wrist, her fake smile falling as soon as Darren turned his head away. He was already pushing through the crowd, and she wriggled through the bodies to keep up, clutching her handbag tightly against her chest. She didn't want to lose him in here, not with this lot. They all looked so strange. Tattoos, piercings, heavy eye make-up and an abundance of black filled her vision in each direction she looked. Did all rock fans dress like this?

She shuddered as she squeezed past a fat, hairy man in leather trousers, grimacing as his belly pressed against her hip. What was she even doing here? This was *so* not her thing.

The theatre, once home to symphony orchestras and Shakespeare plays, had been transformed into what Mia would have imagined one of the seven circles of hell to look like, if she had known about things like that. The graceful Edwardian architecture was lost on her as she was tugged through the herds of people, the sea of murky colours broken only by the peacock-flash of garishly-dyed hair.

Using her bag as a shield, she shoved past a girl with a pierced lip to catch up with Darren, who reached back to pull her closer.

"This way," he grinned, locking her fingers with his. "You're going to love it- you'll see." His enthusiasm was infectious and, despite her misgivings about rock concerts, and the people who frequented them, Mia couldn't help but grin back.

She let herself be jostled into the tight bottle-neck of leather and guyliner that was forming at the doors to the theatre's main hall. It was uncomfortable, to say the least. She tried not to wrinkle her nose at the body odour of the teenage boy wedged against her back, or stare at the facial tattoos of the man who was trying to elbow his way in between Darren and herself. She was *so* out of her depth. The closest she'd come to a rock concert was seeing Busted when she was fourteen. She clung on to Darren's arm as the crush of bodies sealed her in. This was nothing like that.

Darren already had their tickets in his hand, ready to give to the man guarding the single entrance to the main hall. He had a hole in his ear so large that Mia swore she could fit her finger through it. *Didn't that hurt? Who would want to do that to themselves, anyway?* The man caught her staring and Mia blushed, quickly looking away for something- anything- else to gawp at as they shuffled forward.

Her eyes scanned the foyer and rested on a giant poster of

a man wearing a creepy mask complete with goat horns. He was dressed entirely in leather, with a plaited tail that curled around the neck of a young girl who, judging by the look on her face, didn't seem to mind very much that she was being near-strangled, or that she wasn't wearing many clothes. *Maverick Hart*, the poster read. *Rock God Tour, 2013*.

Mia didn't see the fascination, but Darren was such a fanboy; he had all of Maverick's albums and pestered Mia to listen to them too, even making a compilation CD for her of what he considered Maverick Hart's "Greatest Hits" to be. It was a sweet gesture, but Mia preferred normal music, the kind she heard on the radio at work. She played the CD in the car when Darren was there, but she never listened to it when he wasn't around. If she was honest, the screeching guitars gave her a headache, and Maverick's voice gave her nightmares. The lyrics were terrible too- all pseudo-poetry and references to things that Mia would rather not acknowledge. *Weird.*

Still, Darren had been so pleased with himself when he'd presented her with tickets to the *Rock God* tour. Mia could think of a dozen other birthday presents she'd rather have received, but it was too early in their relationship to throw tantrums and, more than that, she didn't want to hurt his feelings. *Thank you*, she'd cooed, wrapping her arms around him. *How thoughtful.* Kate had nearly wet herself when Mia had told her.

"You? At a Maverick Hart gig?" Her flatmate had shaken her head in disbelief. "All that leather and long hair? They're going to eat you alive when you turn up in your heels!" She'd paused there, to hoot with laughter.

Mia didn't think it was *that* funny, and had told her friend so.

"I'm sorry," Kate had spluttered, wiping her eyes. "It's

just that I can't picture you moshing with all the Emos."

Kate had had to explain to Mia what that meant, along with how crowd-surfing worked, and what she should wear. Apparently Mia's usual 'Topshop dress and heels' combo was a no-no. For a group of people who prided themselves on being 'alternative', there were certainly a lot of rules.

Mia fidgeted with the collar of her new t-shirt. It *was* from Topshop, but it had a skull on it, so she thought she'd blend in well enough. It was suitably macabre, she felt, for a gig where the main act cultivated a reputation for all things sinister. She glanced at the poster again and rolled her eyes. *Just weird.*

The mob surged forward, and suddenly they were through the door and in the standing area of the theatre. Darren led her to the side of the room and she followed him gratefully. The standing area was filling up quickly, a restless buzz making the air crackle. Mia hoped they'd just stand at the back to watch- Kate's explanation of mosh-pits hadn't sounded much fun.

"We can see alright from here," Darren assured her. He was practically bouncing with excitement and didn't want her to miss anything. "Do you want your ticket? You know, a souvenir?" He held the stub out to her.

"Yeah, brilliant- thanks." She stuffed it into a side-pocket of her bag and ducked her head through the long strap so it hung across her body. It was more secure that way- another tip from Kate. She craned her neck to see over heads to the front of the hall. The stage was in darkness, the shape of a drum-kit just visible in the shadows. Darren interpreted her action as impatience.

"It'll start any minute now. We can move closer if you like?" His tone was hopeful, but Mia wasn't budging from her spot. Kate had been pretty graphic in her description, even showing her the tooth she'd chipped on someone's boot at a Deftones set back in 2010. She wasn't going anywhere near the mass of bodies that were swarming the floor near the stage- she wanted to stay pretty, thank you very much.

The warm-up band came on, to an appropriately lukewarm response. A crash of chords got the crowd's attention initially but, after a few songs, they became restless and resumed talking amongst themselves. Mia watched them greet each other with bear-hugs and shouts as she sipped from the bottle of vodka she'd hidden in her bag. A few die-hards were rocking out at the front, but the majority were saving their appetites for the main event.

Even from their position at the back of the hall, the music was loud, and Mia had to shout over it to be heard.

"When does Maverick come on?"

"About ten, I think. He likes his audience hungry." Darren winked. "This lot are pretty good, don't you think?"

Mia smiled, her lips tight over her teeth. It just sounded like shouting to her. She checked her watch discreetly. Only twenty-five minutes to go. The sooner it started, the sooner she could go home.

The last minutes crawled by until, finally, a thunderous drum-roll announced the end of the first band's set. Mia shook her head to try and stop the ringing in her ears. *Why did they have to be so loud?* It didn't make them sound any better although, in Mia's opinion, they couldn't have sounded much worse.

The stage crew set up for the main act as more people poured into the crowded room, and Mia, mellowed by the vodka, amused herself by watching the new-comers trying to barge their way to the front. It seemed rude to her, but this was hardly the social scene she was used to. Maybe that kind of behaviour was normal here, along with the weird clothes and hairstyles.

She frowned at herself; she should stop being so judgemental. She was here, so she might as well try and enjoy it. It *did* feel good to be doing something different and, if she went back to the flat saying what a terrible time she'd had, she'd only be confirming Kate's verdict of her being too straight-laced to let her hair down. She mentally shook off her bad mood and made a decision to try harder to get into the spirit of things.

A man in jeans and a *Rock God* tour t-shirt walked onto the stage. He tapped the microphone and coughed nervously.

"Hello!" He flinched visibly as a thousand heads turned in his direction. "Hi. I'm thrilled to announce something very special for you tonight."

He doesn't look thrilled, Mia thought. *He looks terrified*. The thought that she wasn't the only person feeling out of place cheered her, and she tried to look supportively attentive- not that he would have seen her in the throng of faces that eyed him warily.

The man cleared his throat and read from the card he held in his hand. "As you may know, tonight is a very special night for Maverick, and so he has asked me to tell you that he will be selecting a few lucky fans to join him after the show for a special meet-and-greet."

He had the room's attention now, and he began to speak more confidently. "At the end of the show, there will be a board in the foyer with the ticket numbers of the chosen. Please check your stubs and inform a member of staff, who will confirm your winning ticket and escort you backstage to claim your prize."

The room hummed as people digested this. The man waved at the crowd before practically running off into the wings. Mia turned to Darren.

"A meet-and-greet? Does he always do this?" Darren shook his head.

"No, not very often. I've only been to one other show where they held the lottery, and I didn't win. That would have been awesome!"

"Well, if I win, you can have my ticket," Mia offered. Darren laughed.

"Thanks, but there's not much chance of either of us winning. He only ever chooses twelve tickets, and there's over a thousand of us here tonight."

Mia looked around the room at the animated faces; the air buzzed with excited chatter. Any one of these fans would give their right arm to be chosen. It would be kind of cool to meet a real-life 'rock god', and it would certainly make Kate jealous- maybe even stop her teasing- but the thought of being alone with a man who sang about midnight rituals and nefarious deeds made Mia's skin crawl.

Movement on the stage caught her attention and a hush fell over the room as the band took their places, their features indistinguishable in the low light. Every face turned towards the stage, every pair of eyes searching the shadows for a first glimpse of the legendary Maverick Hart.

The anticipation was tangible; Mia's skin tingled with the strength of passion in those around her. Even though this wasn't her thing, it was hard not to get caught up in the mood of the audience. Maybe the vodka had made her brave. She stood on tip-toe, bobbing from side to side to get a better view. Darren grinned at her as the chanting began.

It was like nothing she'd ever experienced. There was something magical in the sound of a thousand voices chanting Maverick's name; it filled the air around her, swelling in volume and urgency, the rhythm both savage and hypnotic. It swept Mia up and, without a conscious decision, she found she was chanting along too. A single spotlight beamed onto the stage, focussed on a microphone stand set in the centre, and the chant grew to a breathless, dizzying roar. The lead guitarist raised his hand and slammed his fingers down in a power-chord. The crowd screamed. The show had begun.

Mia's chest vibrated as the force of the noise slammed into her. The vodka she'd necked churned in her stomach and she clung on to Darren's arm to steady herself, sucking in a deep breath as the roar around her increased.

The band began a furious melody of thrashing guitars and thumping drum beats. The audience howled its approval, all eyes fixed on the stage and the single beam.

The screaming guitars pulverised Mia's brain, making her teeth rattle and her head ache. It was kind of a rush actually, almost fun- if fun involved permanent hearing damage. Her head bobbed with a thousand others, a tightening in her chest sending tingling sensations around her body that pulsed in time with the music. The roar of the fans amplified to unbelievable levels as a lone figure stepped out of the shadows and up to the microphone.

Seeing Maverick Hart, in the flesh, for the first time was electrifying. His hair, wild and luxuriant, fell in a jumble of curls to his bare shoulders, touching the tattoos that ran in sleeves down to his wrists. The skin that wasn't decorated in blue and black swirls glowed a pearlescent ivory, contrasting sharply with the jet-black of his indecently tight trousers. Maverick Hart, the Rock God himself, was stunning to behold.

Mia's heart skipped a beat as Maverick raised one gloved hand to the sky. He held it there for an endless time, teasing the crowd, holding them on the brink, letting their roars of adulation wash over him like a tsunami. He soaked up the adoration, letting it fill him. Finally he leaned forward and snarled into the microphone.

"Prepare to worship…"

The next half hour was a blur to Mia. Adrenalin surged through her body, mingling with the vodka, and she danced and jumped like she had springs on her heels. Maverick was riveting; she'd heard of stage-presence but this guy was a pro. He strutted across the stage like a peacock, proud and in complete control of his congregation, his voice directing their frenzied dance. His low growls made her stomach tighten and, when he belted out the chorus to "Follow Me" she screamed the words along with him, not entirely sure of how she even knew them.

It was incredible. She understood now what she had been missing out on, what Darren had been trying to show her. Maverick Hart was mesmerising- a true Rock God.

Euphoric and light-headed, she grabbed Darren's arm to get his attention and yelled into his ear.

"This is AMAZING!"

Darren hugged her and pulled her towards the mass of writhing bodies.

"I know, right? Feeling brave?"

Mia nodded enthusiastically and plunged into the throng. It was as hot as hell in amongst the other fans, squashed together like marbles in a bean-bag, but she lifted her arms above her head and danced anyway. She was under a spell; *it must be some kind of mass-hysteria*, she thought, grinning at a stranger with a tattooed neck. He grinned back, breaking off only to roar a lyric back at Maverick, who sashayed across the stage like a snake. Mia could barely tear her eyes away from him; he was hypnotising. She jumped higher and higher to snatch glimpses of his tangled black curls over the heads of those in front. The tattooed man motioned with his hands, gesturing up and over the bobbing heads.

"What? Up there?" Mia clapped her hands excitedly and ducked out of her handbag, shoving it at a surprised Darren.

"Mia! No!"

It was too late. Mia stepped onto the man's locked hands and launched herself forwards. She screamed with elation as she was, miraculously as it seemed to her, passed over the heads of the crowd. Dozens- hundreds- of hands held her aloft like some precious cargo; she felt completely safe. She looked up at the ornately-decorated ceiling and hooted as the hands fed her steadily forward towards the stage. She neared the barrier at the front and had a momentary flash of concern. What happened now? How did she get down? She quickly found out. All at once, the hands fell away and she crashed into the arms of a security guard. He dropped her gently to the floor and she leaned on him while she waited for her legs to stop trembling.

She looked back into the crowd, grinning from ear to ear; Darren was out there somewhere, holding her handbag and probably wondering what on earth had come over his girlfriend. She giggled at her own daring. Even she wasn't sure what had happened. It must be the music, the crowd- *him*. The hairs on the back of her neck stood up and she spun round to face the stage.

Maverick was barely metres from her, singing into the microphone he held in his left hand. His right hand was pointing straight at her. Their eyes locked in an unending moment and Mia felt the world tilt and twist around her; he was reading her soul, invading her head and filling it with wild thoughts. He was singing only to her- and she liked it.

"Come on, love." The security guard lifted her up and carried her off to the side of the stage. She felt the wrench as she lost eye-contact with Maverick, but there was no chance of getting back to him now. The guard dropped her over a barrier and she was back in the main hall with the other fans. She stood, dazed and breathless, reliving those precious seconds. He had stared into her eyes and spoken to her. Maverick Hart- Rock God. She understood why women became groupies; his charisma was addictive.

"Mia!" Darren appeared by her side, grabbing her arm and shaking her out of her stupor. He was laughing, but even Mia's fuddled brain could detect the concern on his face. "You're mental! Crowd-surfing?" He wrapped her in a tight hug and spoke into her ear. "I'm so glad you're ok, and that you're having a good time- but please don't scare me like that again." He led her to the back of the room, edging around the thrashing dancers. Mia sat on a step and caught her breath.

"Wow. I can't believe I just did that!" She shook her head and laughed. She felt energised, like she could dance and run and sing forever. She took a few swigs of what was left of the vodka, offering the last drops to Darren, who drained the bottle and placed it on the floor next to the wall. Jumping to her feet, she grabbed Darren's hand and pulled him towards the crowd. "Let's go back!"

Darren followed her. "No more running off though." They re-joined the dancing devotees, but this time Darren stayed close.

Too soon for Mia, the last chorus was sung, the music stopped and, with a final triumphant wave to the faithful, Maverick left the stage. Darren took Mia's hand as the lights were turned up and they followed the euphoric and sweaty crowd out into the foyer.

"So, you enjoyed it then?"

Mia's eyes sparkled as she nodded enthusiastically.

"It was mega! I didn't realise how amazing he is. I mean-" Mia frowned as she tried to find the words to explain the overwhelming emotion she had experienced. "-he really is awesome. A Rock *God*. I feel so..." She couldn't explain it. It was like she'd been shown another world, one where she was more than a dental-hygienist who holidayed in Ibiza and worried about her cellulite. Tonight she'd felt wild, free- released from a cage.

Darren squeezed her fingers, pleased.

"I knew you'd think so. It's so different seeing him live to just listening to the CD- you can really appreciate his genius when you see him in the flesh."

"Yeah." Mia recalled the way Maverick's eyes had stared into her own and shivered. They had a shared a moment, she was sure of it.

"Look," Darren pointed over to where a group had gathered. "There's the board. Let's check our tickets." They queued to get close enough to read the numbers. Darren scanned the board and shook his head.

"No, not mine. What about yours?" Mia unzipped the pocket of her bag and pulled out her ticket to compare the number with those hand-written on the board.

"No," she said. "I don't think- wait!" She checked them again, her hands shaking slightly. She looked at Darren, her eyes wide. "My number's on the board!"

"No way! You get to meet him!" Darren took the ticket out of her fingers and read the numbers, a delighted smile spreading across his lips. "I don't believe it- you're so jammy. Your first ever gig and you win the lottery." He handed back her ticket, crumpling his own into a ball. Mia felt bad. Darren was hiding it well, but he was disappointed. He wanted this so much; he'd been a fan for so much longer. It didn't seem fair.

"You have it," she said. "I'm only here because of you, and you've always wanted to meet him." She held the ticket stub out to him. Darren shook his head.

"No. It's your ticket- you should go. It was your birthday present." Mia tried not to look too pleased. As much as she wanted Darren to be happy, meeting Maverick was going to be *epic*.

"If you're sure..." Darren nodded and Mia, secretly gleeful, looked around for where she needed to go.

She held up her ticket to a staff member and was shown out of the foyer and into a long corridor that led to the backstage area. The room was full of plush, red leather sofas and chairs, organised into small huddles around low tables. Four girls were already waiting there, and seven more joined them after Mia had chosen a seat. They were all, including Mia, in their late-teens, early twenties- and all obviously female. *Strange... what were the odds of all the chosen tickets belonging to girls?* It had seemed, to Mia, that the majority of the audience were male. Mia shrugged mentally. Maybe they'd begged their boyfriends to swap, as she probably would have done. She checked her make-up quickly, zipped up her bag and crossed her legs, swinging her foot as the minutes ticked by.

Finally, the door opened.

Mia sat up straight as Maverick entered the room, wearing a long, black silk robe and nothing on his feet. His hair lay in damp ringlets across his shoulders. She couldn't see what- if anything- he was wearing underneath and a thrill danced over her skin. He motioned for them to relax.

"Ladies," he greeted them with a wolfish smile. "Welcome, and thank you. It's an honour to meet my devotees, the faithful." His eyes swept across the faces, settling on Mia's for a second longer than the others. A spark of desire made Mia jump in her seat.

"Please, help yourself to drinks and nibbles. You must be in need of sustenance after all that effort. I know I'm ravenous." He licked his lips to emphasise the point, his eyes flickering back to Mia. A tray of drinks was presented by an anonymous waiter and Mia picked a glass at random. She gulped it while she thought desperately of something to say. The fizzy liquid tasted bitter, but she wasn't much of a wine drinker, so she couldn't complain. Maybe it was supposed to taste like that.

Maverick moved between the winners, laughing, chatting, signing shirts. Mia's heart began to pound as her turn neared. Would he remember her? Her brain was fuzzy- whatever had been in her now-empty glass had been strong, and was sitting on a good half-pint of vodka. She hoped she wouldn't say or do anything stupid- Kate and Darren would never forgive her.

Maverick finished with the leggy blonde in a tight top and turned to Mia. He pulled up a chair and sat back in it.

"Hi." His voice was melodious and soft. He took the empty glass from her and placed it on the table before taking her hand in his. "You're the girl from before- the one who came over the barrier and landed at my feet." He smiled, his sable eyes twinkling. "How strange that destiny should choose your ticket tonight." His beautiful face blurred as he leaned closer to whisper in her ear. "Tell me, do you believe in fate?"

"Umm... I'm not really sure." Mia blushed. Why was she so slow? She racked her brains for something witty or clever with which to reply. "I think belief in the thing itself makes it powerful."

Where had *that* come from? Maverick seemed to like it though. He tilted his head back and laughed, a hearty chuckle that warmed Mia's cheeks even more. The other girls stared cattily at her, none of them had made him laugh like that.

He patted her knee. "Wise words, indeed. And truer than most would credit." He cocked his head to the side. "Tell me your name, wise one."

"Mia." She blinked slowly. Why did she feel so dizzy all of a sudden?

Maverick repeated the word, rolling it around his mouth like he was tasting the sound. It made Mia's head spin even faster.

"Well, Mia," he said, savouring her name again, "I'm most grateful to the gods of destiny that we met tonight."

Mia heard the words through a hazy fog of background noise. The room was spiralling, and tight spasms gripped her stomach.

"I- I'm sorry." Nausea washed over Mia like a wave. "I feel a bit... strange." Maverick released her hand and waved over a tall man.

"Marcus, take Mia into the other room and lay her down. I think she's a little overwhelmed."

Was it her imagination, or did a look of understanding flash between the two men? Mia opened her mouth to protest as two strong arms lifted her but her words turned into a mumble and she was carried through the door Maverick had emerged from into a larger, cooler room, the conversations popping like bubbles of sound in her ears as they grew fainter.

The man laid her down on a suede sofa, which felt too hot under her clammy skin. The light from the single lamp was feeble, but too bright for her eyes so she closed them, just for a moment, until the feeling of sickness passed. Her limbs felt weak, she could barely move her arm to raise her hand to her brow and wipe away the sheen of perspiration.

Maybe she had overdone it- the heat, the dancing, the alcohol. How embarrassing though, to swoon in front of Maverick Hart like some giddy groupie. Poor Darren; she'd left him waiting in the foyer for too long- he'd be worried.

Mia moaned, mortified at how the evening had turned out. She needed to get it together, sort herself out and get out of there. Eyes still closed, she swung her legs off the sofa and pushed herself into a sitting position. Using her arms to brace herself and stay upright, she took a few deep breaths. The room was silent; not even a sound from beyond the closed door. She didn't remember the tall man closing it- hadn't heard him leave. She should go; Darren would fret if she didn't return soon. She steadied her legs, ready to stand.

"Welcome back, Mia."

She squeaked in surprise. The voice, coming from the shadows in the corner of the dimly-lit room, chuckled at her reaction. She squinted to make out the owner.

"Who's that?" she rasped, her mouth sticky, like she'd been asleep. The shadows stirred and a figure strode into the light. Maverick Hart still wore his robe and his bare feet made no sound as he crossed the room and sat next to her on the sofa. Mia could just make out his eyes, intense and hungry as they lingered over her face. He reached out and stroked her hair, tucking a tendril behind her ear with fingers that were hot on her cheek, as if fire burned beneath his skin.

"So delicious," he whispered. "I was hoping it would be you. You don't know how glad I am that you chose this."

Mia was confused. *Chose this?* She leaned away from him and tried to stand, but her legs were like jelly and wouldn't support her. Maverick sighed happily and took her chin in his hand, turning her head until she had no alternative but to look at him. His face was not as beautiful as she'd remembered; his skin more sallow in this light, the texture rough like tree-bark. His teeth were uneven and sharp. She recoiled but he held her tight.

"You are displeased? And I thought I looked pretty good for my age."

"Your age?" *What was he on about?* "How old are you?"

"Older than you could imagine." Maverick smiled but the warmth didn't reach his eyes. "I am older than Mankind."

What a ridiculous thing to say. Mia wondered if he was on drugs. He had a wild look in his eyes, a coiled tension to his movements- as if he were wound up tight and ready to pounce. A chill ran through her as she remembered the drink she had taken, and her sudden illness. Had he drugged her? Where was everyone else?

She leaned forward, using gravity to shift off the sofa and stumble to the door. It was locked. She thumped it a few times before her legs gave way and she slid down to the ground. She twisted on the floor so she was facing him, trying not to panic. She was trapped. Maverick eyed her coolly, an amused expression on his face. He hadn't moved from the sofa.

"There is no use running. The poison still runs through your veins, and there is nowhere to go." Maverick paused to let his statement to sink in. "You might as well sit down here and rest." He patted the sofa invitingly. "Then I can tell you a story before I devour your heart."

A finger of ice ran up and down Mia's spine. *Poison?* He was obviously insane or on something. What should she do? Her eyes darted around the room, searching for an escape route, but the only way out was through the locked door she leant against. She thought of Darren, waiting for her in the foyer. How long had she been here? He'd come looking for her soon. She just had to keep Maverick talking until then, distract him from doing anything… stupid. She kept her voice as calm as his when she replied.

"I'm fine here," she said evenly, her racing heartbeat proving her a liar. "Tell me your story."

Maverick shrugged.

"As you choose." He stood up and crossed the room. Mia watched curiously as he took a candle from a carved wooden box on the table in the corner. He spoke softly as he lit the candle with a match, the flame dancing as it spluttered into life.

"Before there was mankind, there was me. I lived in the forests, skulking silently amongst the already ancient trees, preying on the weak and vulnerable creatures. I crept up to them while they slept, whispered in their ears, before they even understood the meaning of the words. I devoured their terrified hearts when they strayed too deep into my realm, savouring the taste. I stole into their dreams and filled their heads with dread and violence. They heard me and trembled- and their fear made me stronger."

He blew out the match and carried the candle over to Mia, setting it down on the floor at her feet. The candle's glow lit his face from below, twisting his features into something wicked. He stooped suddenly and grabbed a fistful of her hair, ignoring her squeals as he plucked a single one.

"I stalked Men in my forests, feeding on their flesh and fright."

Just as quickly, he released her. Mia rubbed the painful spot on her scalp and watched, open-mouthed, as he held the single strand over the flame until it smoked and disintegrated, the foul smell making her cough when it reached her. Maverick inhaled deeply, eyes closed as he wafted the acrid smoke towards his face.

"Interesting..." He opened his eyes, smiled and brushed off his fingers before taking a seat on the sofa and leaning back leisurely.

"They learnt to avoid the sunless places, to be afraid of them," he continued, as if nothing strange had just happened. "Over time, I watched the men rise from their bellies and stand, tall and proud. I watched the first hunt. The men were brutal but disorganised. They lacked leadership. I realised they had potential, these apes with cruel hearts- and so I decided to train them.

The flickering shadows in the corners of the room began to swirl. Maverick continued, unaware or uncaring as they grew darker, more solid.

"I followed one of the tribe on a hunt; he was the strongest, the fastest and the one I wanted. I appeared to him, as he was finishing off a kill, taking on a form that struck fear into his heart."

Mia's eyes widened in horror as Maverick's face transformed. Blood filled his cheeks in thick stripes and his eyes blackened until no white could be seen. His hair twisted up on itself until it formed tight cords like the roots of ancient oaks. *How did he do that?* She rubbed her eyes, but when she opened them that hideous face was still gazing down at her, lips twisted into a grim parody of pleasure.

"Yes, he was afraid- as afraid as you are now. He pleaded with me silently, pushing the deer between himself and me. I spared him, and fed on the deer's flesh instead. I had patience, and a grander plan. As I predicted, the man returned to the same spot the next day with another deer and we came to an arrangement. Our bargain was sealed in blood." His grin stretched at the memory. "My first tribute."

Mia shivered and drew her feet up, away from the shadowy fingers that stretched across the floor towards her. She kept her eyes on them as she listened, unable to look at the hideous creature in front of her.

"I took my place as their leader. My pets learned fast and added their own savagery. I approved. The tribe grew stronger, larger. I helped them crawl out of the swamp and dust- and they were grateful." He leant forward and fixed his gaze on Mia, his black eyes sparkling with memories of his past glory.

"In return for my protection and restraint, they brought me gifts. Every day I feasted on the deer and other animals they laid at my feet in tribute. I had never fed so well, or so regularly. My power grew even stronger, fuelled by their offerings and sacrifices. I solidified from shadow to idol. The gifts grew more precious as they reached for greater things."

Maverick waved his hand and the shadows pulled away from Mia, stretching up to form human figures that knelt and held out shapeless bundles. She watched, horrified, as they acted out Maverick's words, a hideous tableau of a long-forgotten history. Was she hallucinating? She blinked and tried to focus on them, but they twitched and danced away, lingering on the edge of her vision.

"My tastes grew more refined; I got fussy," Maverick continued. "When I fed on their fear, it was like drinking from muddy pools, the taste tainted with the terror of my victims."

The shadows screamed silently in response. Maverick laughed softly, his eyes as murky as a moonless sky.

"But when I fed on their awe, it was like supping from a mountain stream, the flavour pure and sweet with their longing."

It was the intensity of his gaze that stirred a flicker of belief in Mia's heart, the absolute sincerity of his voice that convinced her. He was remembering, not inventing; he wasn't crazy, he was... something else. It made no sense at all, went against everything the modern world had taught her-but it was somehow true. Maverick Hart was a God, an old god, returned from the legends that had become fiction.

The scale of the danger she was in hit Mia and she choked back a sob. He really was going to devour her heart- unless Darren hurried up. She had to keep him talking. She swallowed a whimper and nodded encouragingly for him to continue, though she trembled at the thought of what he might reveal next.

Maverick resumed his story.

"I learned, over time, that adoration is like the finest wine, far superior, intoxicating even. I developed a taste for strong flesh and pure hearts. I no longer settled for the blood of animals. I deserved more- and they complied."

A gasp escaped Mia's lips as she realised what he meant. Maverick saw her shocked expression and nodded.

"Yes. Human sacrifice." He waited a moment to allow the words to be absorbed fully. "With my assistance and guidance, they defeated neighbouring tribes and converted them, bringing the strongest of their enemies for me to feed on." He winked. "Defiance has its own flavour."

The shadows changed and became giants, falling to their knees and throwing their heads back to roar at the sky. Mia trembled as one by one they were slain. She turned her face away, looking down at the floor to avoid the nightmarish visions, and spotted something small and dark, tucked under the sofa.

Her handbag, dropped and forgotten by Marcus when he'd laid her down.

Mia's breath caught in her throat; her phone was in there! She just had to reach it without him seeing. She kept her face blank as she looked away quickly, not wanting him to realise what had caught her attention.

Maverick waited until she raised her head before speaking

STRANGE IDEAS: DEATH, DESTINY AND DECISIONS

again.

"Each year I grew stronger, more powerful, more adored. Your lives are so brief, but I remember it all: when chiefs and leaders bowed to me and begged my favour, offering up the best of their kingdoms in tribute to me..." His mighty voice trailed away, sorrow etched in the lines on his brow. Just for a moment, he looked pathetic- pitiful even.

He had had everything, Mia thought, *and had lost it all*.

She found her voice at last, although she took care to make it respectful; she didn't want to anger him.

"If you were once so powerful, why are you here now- like this? Why aren't you running the country or something?"

Maverick shook his head ruefully.

"I took on the ways and wiles of man; I became greedy, lustful, engorged by their worship. My power was so strong, their belief in me so absolute, that I became complacent." His eyes darkened, the black pools swirling in anger.

"As a millennium of seasons passed, routines formed. The rituals became more formal, their original purpose lost in pomp and pageantry. It outgrew me, until I became superfluous to the ceremony. Men no longer feared me, they... humoured me."

Maverick's mouth twisted in a grimace and he ran his fingers through his hair in agitation. Mia backed away as far as the locked door would allow her as the twisted curls sprang back into shape, quivering with a life of their own.

"With the progress of man, came the destruction of the forests. My kingdom shrank as men moved into the clear spaces and built settlements and towns, cities with bright lights and no shadows to placate. With the loss of followers, of *belief*, my strength waned."

He clenched his fists and glared into the past, spitting the words.

"Too much magic, too many charismatic charlatans with fancy robes and mystical sticks; they took what was once a pure, albeit mercenary, arrangement and twisted it to suit their own lust for power. Like they had once listened to me, men now hung on *their* every word. True belief in me dwindled, and with it, my influence.

"Strange men came, with a new god and a hatred of the old ways. My 'faithful' were now only old women huddled around fires during a full moon, mumbling words that meant little to me. The sacrifices became token gestures to appease a dying deity who was too weak to act."

He sighed and fell back onto the sofa. The shadows ebbed in response. His voice became flat and devoid of emotion, barely a murmur, and Mia strained to hear his next words.

"I shrank back into the shadows and watched my empire crumble. I lurked, barely existing, on the edge of the forest for many lifetimes of man, remembered only in legends and warnings to those who strayed too deep into my realm." His head drooped.

Mia edged her feet out, testing the strength of her legs. Her handbag was tantalisingly close- it would take only seconds to fling herself across the room and reach it. The wooziness was easing; the poison- whatever it was- that had been in her drink was wearing off, although she still felt weak She needed to keep him talking until she was sure she could outrun him.

Also, she had to admit she was intrigued. If what he told her was true, then how could he exist in a modern world full of science, where belief no longer existed and proof was everything?

"How- how did you recover?" she asked.

Maverick raised his head and their eyes locked. Mia held his gaze bravely.

STRANGE IDEAS: DEATH, DESTINY AND DECISIONS

"I thought that my power was gone forever," he sighed, "until one day, I sensed a huge amount of adoration, heard a swelling of voices lifted in worship. I crept closer to the source. A man, just a mortal, stood on a stage in a field. He sang, and the crowd sang with him, pouring out their hearts in his honour. I realised what I must do. Just like men, I had to adapt to survive, to learn about this strange new world and find my place in it. I changed my form. I adapted. I adopted this new world and its new customs. I was reborn."

His face became softer, more attractive. His eyes lost their glassy blackness and his hair fell once more in soft curls that begged to be stroked. This was the seductive form he had chosen in order to bewitch a new generation of worshippers, Mia realised. It had been effective.

"I became Maverick Hart."

The pieces fell into place in Mia's head. Hadn't she read something just the other day about celebrity being the new religion? People didn't go to church anymore; they went to the cinema. They didn't seek advice from priests or holy texts- they sought it from chat-show hosts and gossip magazines. The Ten Commandments had been replaced by Vogue's Ten Best Dressed list. It was easy to find believers in a society that searched for someone to follow, who discarded the rules their grandparents had lived by and created their own. She nodded. She understood.

"You became a celebrity."

"And they worshipped me again." He pulled something from the sleeve of his robe- leaves, Mia thought, though of what sort, she couldn't tell- and began to shred them into thin strips with his fingers. "The groupies fell over themselves to offer up their bodies to me. They nourished me but left a bad taste in my mouth." He plaited the strips together as he spoke. "It was too easy, and I'd had better.

Where is the value in a prize so easily won?"

He knelt down on the floor and held the plaited rod over the flame. It popped and cracked before turning to ash, which fell and mixed in with the liquid wax, creating a black circle at the base of the wick. The colour was almost as gloomy as the shadows that waited, biding their time, in the corners of the room.

"As I regained my strength, I ascended to larger establishments: theatres, concert halls, festivals and arenas. My worshippers grew younger, firmer, more succulent. I feasted again, though not as often. Regular worship, or gigs as you would call them, sustained me between sacrifices."

The sick sense of dread in Mia's stomach returned.

"You *feed* on your fans? But that's monstrous!"

"You didn't object when I told you about the human sacrifices before." A smirk pulled the corner of his mouth as he eyed her hungrily.

"That was different! That was back in the dark ages- we don't sacrifice people anymore! We don't-"

Maverick silenced her with a curl of his fingers. Mia clutched her throat, struggling to breathe. He dipped his index finger into the pool of black wax and leaned forward to smear a pattern across her forehead and cheeks, dipping his finger again to collect more with which to draw a line down her throat. The wax stung with more than heat; it was a brand, a mark of ownership.

Maverick rested back on his heels and slowly uncurled his fist to release her windpipe. Mia sucked in breaths of smoky air, inhaling the heady fumes from the candle and wincing at the fire of the wax and the ice in his voice.

"Maybe you should have done it more often," he sneered. "Your society's lack of commitment to faith is the reason it is failing. Do you not wonder that, while churches crumble, ever-larger shopping centres are built? That congregations dwindle while social networks flourish? Mankind needs to be led, to conform. With no leadership, you revert back to the swamp-creatures I observed many thousands of years ago."

He leapt to his feet and paced back and forth, speaking passionately as Mia tried to rub the wax from her face and chest. She scratched at it with her fingernails, but it soaked into her skin instead of laying on top.

"You think you are rebelling against the system, against your parent's values, deliberately living your lives on the edge of society. I have always lived on the edge, between day and night, revenge and mercy, passion and terror. This democratic world you inhabit serves my purpose more completely than any dictatorship I could have devised. To collect together in worship of a man on a stage is to conform."

He halted abruptly and gazed down at Mia, who cowered from the mockery in his eyes. She saw herself as he did, a naïve little girl who followed the herd. A sheep. A lamb to be slaughtered.

"My image adorns a million walls," he whispered. "A million voices gather to sing praise to me. A million worshippers crave my audience. A million of the fittest, strongest, most beautiful, most *precious* line up to sacrifice themselves-"

His lip curled contemptuously.

"-and they come willingly. They flock here, not in fear or greed, but in adoration and worship, and each of their own free will."

He glowered at her, daring her to challenge him. Mia could not. Terror thrummed in her veins. He knelt down, hissing the next words only centimetres from her face.

"I've watched warriors weep, seen first-born sons fight their fate. This is much easier. This is their choice. *Your* choice. You came here enthusiastically, as they have all done. You claimed your ticket and left your- friend- and didn't look back. You were not dragged here, rebellious and unwilling."

Mia opened her mouth to protest, but the truth silenced her.

Maverick leaned closer to deliver his final blow. "Don't tell me that you did not choose this, that you are not here of your own free will. Your decisions are your own- even down to choosing the one glass of wine that was laced with mistletoe."

His face was so close to hers she could feel the tickle of his stubble on her cheek, and his breath was sour, rotten in her nostrils. Her time had run out- *where was Darren?* Mia shut her eyes and steeled herself for the pounce, her heart thudding loudly in her ears and her lips moving as she prayed for a swift death. Maverick tensed, ready to claim his tribute.

From under the sofa, Mia's phone began to ring. Both their heads whipped towards the sound, Maverick's focus off her for just the second Mia needed. Renewed hope and adrenalin pumped through her body. This was her chance.

Mia lashed out, taking him by surprise and clawing his face with her nails. She scrabbled to her knees as he reeled back. Panting with the effort of escaping, she crawled towards her handbag, her feeble legs pushing against the wooden floor. The ringing was like a beacon, and she swam towards it through the dizziness and paralysing panic. Her fingers closed around her bag's thin strap and she pulled it towards her, fingers desperately searching for the zip. Maybe it was Darren, or Kate- someone who could save her from this monster of nightmares. She almost had it-

Maverick howled and leapt on her back, knocking her to the floor and hurling her bag away to be engulfed by the murky shadows, the phone still trilling its merry tune. He turned Mia over and pinned her to the ground with one hand, the other clutching his cheek. Thick red blood oozed from between his fingers and dripped onto her skull t-shirt.

Mia screamed and tried to wriggle out from beneath him, hand stretching to reach the candle, but he pressed down on her ribs, the accelerated thud of her heart striking his palm as if even that part of her fought him. She pinched and scratched the skin on his arm, but it was as hard as oak. Her phone fell finally silent, her last hope of rescue gone.

Maverick laughed as he swung his leg over to sit astride her, his hands holding down her arms easily, his stringy hair hanging down onto her face.

Triumphant, he ran his nose across the wax on her forehead and neck, breathing in the aroma.

"Defiance has its own flavour," he repeated, his lips drawn back to reveal the daggers that filled his mouth. "Darren chose well this time. He will be richly rewarded. Even though you are not one of the faithful, you will still taste sweet."

The scream died in Mia's throat and was replaced with a terrified whimper as the extent of Darren's betrayal sank in. It all made sense now: his eagerness for her to come tonight, his insistence that she keep her ticket and claim her "prize". He had tricked her into being here, sacrificed her to his idol in exchange for- what? She looked up at Maverick, his eyes lit with demonic fire and mouth already salivating, and knew that she would never find out the price for her life, that in seconds it would be over.

Her last thought before Maverick swooped down and sank his teeth into her flesh was that she should have guessed.

After all, Darren was such a fanboy.

SUPERSTITION

Yanked from her pleasant dream by the scream of her alarm clock, Laura rolled over and slapped the "off" button down with more force than was necessary, her eyes still half-closed. She scowled sleepily, dreading the moment when she must open her eyes fully and acknowledge the day. Serious considerations of hitting "snooze" crossed her mind, but then the alarm would sound again at 7:06, and that would never do. The lovely images faded as real life elbowed its way into her conscious mind. She sighed. She hated Fridays.

Moving stealthily so as not to wake the slumbering form next to her, she rolled out of bed on the right side and slid her feet into her slippers: right foot first, then the left. Always the same. She stumbled groggily towards the bathroom, occasionally ricocheting from the walls and various items of furniture, counting her steps as she went. Eighteen. This was good.

In the bathroom, Laura washed her face and brushed her teeth, making sure to perform each action an even number of times. She screwed up her face while she brushed, trying and failing to count the lines that appeared beside her eyes. Each day, there seemed to be another. She frowned at herself in the mirror, contorting her pretty face until it resembled the crumpled duvet she'd left behind. Her ash-blonde hair looked

STRANGE IDEAS: DEATH, DESTINY AND DECISIONS

grey in the artificial light, her skin pale and washed-out, like the colour had been leeched from her. She felt drained too; living like this was exhausting.

Laura spat, rinsed her toothbrush and wiped her mouth, being careful to leave the towel folded neatly on the rail. She returned to the bedroom- fourteen steps this time, which was even better- to dress.

Today would require something special. She selected the skirt that she had been wearing the day she passed her driving test and the V-neck jumper she had been wearing when Brighton won against Leyton Orient in 2011. It was a beautiful cerulean blue that stood out against the more neutral-toned hues in her wardrobe, but she needed something bold today, something lucky. Today was going to be a good day; she'd make sure of it.

She slid a silver bangle -a present from her first boyfriend- over her wrist, glancing guiltily at her husband behind her. He slept, stagnant, sprawled out across the mattress, taking up more room than was fair. She shook her head to dislodge the unkind thoughts that suddenly shouted their outrage. That wouldn't do; she shouldn't think bad things.

She checked her reflection in the full-length mirror hanging on the bedroom wall; she looked smart, assured- exactly the image she wanted to project to the watching world. It wouldn't do to let anyone know. Satisfied, she tip-toed round to the wrong side of the bed and kissed the still-sleeping figure on the cheek. He stirred, grunting dozily, but did not wake. His face was peaceful, oblivious to the countdown before his alarm woke him.

"I love you," she whispered. She never left him without saying it, even now, just in case. Adam snored gently in reply. She closed the bedroom door quietly before descending the stairs, right foot first, and making her way to the kitchen.

SUPERSTITION

The pale green walls glowed softly in the shards of light slipping through the blinds, the counters gleamed and the appliances shone. *Show-home perfect*, Adam complained, but Laura liked it that way. She pulled up the blinds to let the bright spring sunshine flood in and began to prepare her breakfast, each movement automatic from routine.

She boiled the kettle and poured it over the teabag, being sure to stir the spoon clockwise. As she poured in the milk, she was pleased to see dozens of tiny bubbles on the surface of her tea. This was good. Bubbles meant money coming her way. Goodness knows, she needed it. With Adam out of work for so long, it was becoming increasingly difficult to make the little money she earned stretch to cover everything.

Work-shy swine.

She threw the spoon in the sink, taking her flash of anger out on the stainless steel. It bounced in the grey bowl with a dull drum-roll of thuds. She immediately felt guilty again. She shouldn't think like that. It wasn't his fault.

Adam had been ambitious, a "bright young thing", when she'd met him. She'd lost her heart to his charm and her own dreams to the pursuit of his. She'd left her friends, family and everyone she knew to move down to London so he could take up a position as a city banker. She'd regretted it ever since.

Her anger, though quickly banished, hung over her like a bad omen. She was distracted, and narrowly avoided an incident while making her toast. As she was buttering the second slice, the knife slipped from her fingers and fell to the floor, clattering against the stone tiles. She swore and froze, ears straining for any indication that the sound had woken him. Long seconds passed before she felt safe; he hadn't heard it.

She looked down at the knife, lying like it had been

abandoned by a fleeing attacker. There was no one there to pick it up for her, so she would have to do it herself. This was not good. She turned around and stepped backwards over the knife before she picked it up and dropped it in the sink, next to the tea spoon. That should cancel out the bad luck. Laura tutted. She hoped it wasn't going to be one of those days.

She sipped her tea and munched on her toast in the dining room, looking out into the untidy garden, enjoying the peace and listening to the wood pigeons calling to each other. Today would be a stressful one. Fridays usually were, but this one would be worse than normal. She relished the calm before the storm, wishing she could ask for some overtime and avoid the long weekend at home altogether, but she knew she couldn't. He wouldn't like it. Maybe she could do some gardening, stay away from him outside the whole time; it certainly needed some tidying, and there was no point in asking Adam to do it while she was at work. Yes, that's what she'd do. She nodded happily to herself, swallowed the last of her tea and got ready to leave.

Laura smiled back at the sun as she stepped out of the house and began her walk to work. She could have driven, but it was only a short distance and she enjoyed walking- enjoyed any reason for being out of the house in fact. Besides, she couldn't afford to waste petrol, not this week. She readjusted the position of her handbag, her purse safe inside, her money safe inside that, and tried not to feel guilty. It was *her* money, after all.

Reaching into her pocket, she pulled out her old and slightly battered iPod and selected "shuffle". The first song to come on was "Smile" by Lily Allen. This was good, so she did indeed smile as she strolled. She was in no particular hurry today and she needed time to think.

SUPERSTITION

Last night had been difficult. She had been late home from work, something she tried her best to avoid. He hadn't liked it. *It's bad enough that you're the only one earning,* he'd ranted, the pub-lunch slurring his words and hardening his eyes, *without rubbing it in by swanning home whenever you feel like it.* She'd tried to soothe him, apologise, make it better, but he'd pushed her away before storming back out, probably to the pub. She'd made herself beans on toast and eaten them in her dressing gown, ashamed at how much she'd enjoyed the evening alone. It wasn't often she had time to herself now.

Back when Adam had been employed, he'd worked long hours, and stayed even longer to drink with his new friends. A kept woman- his choice, not hers- Laura had sat at home in their flat, alone in the big city, and dreamed of another life. She'd spent her days cleaning, rearranging and titivating until everything was just so, the only part of her life left where she had control. That was when it had started, she supposed- the counting, the checking, the rituals and superstitions. The doctor called it OCD; Adam called her a freak. She knew better.

The path by the police-station took a while to negotiate as there were so many cracks to avoid but she made good time and was soon on the main road. The cars zoomed past her, the noise of their engines drowned out by Counting Crow's "Mr Jones". She was alert as she walked, as always, watching carefully for any trouble that she could avoid, but the happy song protected her. "Shuffle" was on her side today. This was good. She needed everything to go her way today, if she was to be successful.

She'd been asleep when he'd returned last night. His stumbling and swearing had woken her, and she'd tried not to tense her body as he climbed the stairs. He'd been spoiling for a fight all week, and she didn't want anything bad to happen. He didn't hit her- not since that one time- but he hurt her in other ways, with stinging words and insults that didn't leave marks where anyone would see. Luckily, his anger had been diluted by all the beer, and he'd thrown himself into bed without comment, rolling over and taking most of the duvet with him. She'd slept fitfully, shivering occasionally but not daring to reclaim her share of the cover in case she woke him and it began again. Sometimes it felt like all she did was appease him. On bad days, she hated him for it; the rest of the time, she hated herself for putting up with it.

She turned left just past the post office and cut down the alleyway that was always lined with wildflowers. She liked to see them, sheltered from the elements and stretching up to the narrow strip of sun. It reminded her that there was light and beauty in even the drabbest of corners: that even the weeds had something to live for. She craned her head back to let the rays fall on her face, imagining that she too was wild and self-sufficient. It felt good, even though it wasn't true.

She emerged from the alley and crossed the road to avoid a black cat that crouched, hissing at her, on the pavement. Laura would have hissed back, except someone might have seen. Time and taunts had taught her to keep her superstitions to herself; other people, those that didn't understand, flapped them away as old-wives tales. She knew better, of course, but there was no use in trying to explain it to them. She kept an eye on the cat and counted in her head as she drew level, worried that it would approach her. She stopped counting and relaxed her shoulders only as she passed it.

She didn't have a problem with other animals; in fact, just last week she'd seen a puppy advertised in the newsagent where she always bought the weekend paper, the one luxury she allowed herself. A beautiful Cavalier boy, so small he looked like a toy rather than a living creature. He had chocolate-brown eyes and tiny paws that were barely bigger than the thumbs of the faceless person who held him up to pose for the camera. She hadn't even been looking; the card had fallen from the board as she'd opened the door, letting the cold gusts in with her. It had fallen at her feet as if wanting to be seen: a Sign. She'd picked it up to replace it and fallen in love immediately.

She'd asked him that night, her husband, and he had sneered at her, his lips curling derisively. *Oh great, another thing for me to worry about,* he'd drawled sarcastically. *You think I've got nothing better to do, just because I don't have a job? Who's going to clean up after it while you're at work?* She'd had to bite her tongue to reply that actually, no, she didn't think he did very much all day except sign on and go to the pub, and that owning a dog was something that would make her happy and, after all, it would be *her* money paying for it. She didn't dare say any of that. She'd not mentioned it again, and now the card was gone. Adam was so selfish, so heartless. Sometimes she hated him.

She shook her head quickly; she shouldn't think like that. Bad thoughts made bad things happen, and today was going to be a good day- a *lucky* day. As if on cue, a magpie landed in the hedge. She nodded three times and wished him good morning before she continued on her way. He cocked his head to watch her pass, approving. She checked her watch; even with taking the scenic route, she was on time. This was good. She joined the road that led to her office.

After a blazing row with Adam, one of the few of their married life, she had applied for a part-time job as a secretary, just for something to do. It wasn't a challenge, not with her degree, but thank goodness she had. Adam was one of the first to go in the purge following the banking scandal, a scapegoat offered up as a sacrifice to the public, out-of-pocket and baying for blood. It wasn't that he'd done anything wrong- she frowned and rephrased the thought more truthfully- he hadn't done any *more* wrong than the others, but the old-boy network had closed ranks and pushed him onto the scrapheap. She'd felt guilty, though Adam scoffed. She knew it was her fault, really.

They'd left the flat and moved somewhere smaller, cheaper, and closer to her work; somewhere the neighbours changed on a monthly basis and the bin men felt safer working in packs. She'd asked to increase her hours at the office to full-time, just to make ends meet and, luckily, her boss had agreed. Adam had point-blank refused to get a job he considered beneath him, even when his pay-off ran out. *I'm not one of those blue-collar plebs*, he'd laughed scornfully. *I'm holding out for something decent*. But nothing was ever good enough, and now unemployment had become a habit. The anger bubbled again and she fought to control it. She shouldn't think bad things. It wouldn't do.

But she couldn't go on like this, with Adam. She had to do something.

She needed to detour round some scaffolding at the corner before she could enter her building. It had been there for weeks now, an ugly exoskeleton attached to the estate agents that had once been a pub. Laura wondered when they would ever be finished, as there never seemed to be any workmen actually working on anything. She felt, on bad days, that they were camped there to torment her, leaving ladders to trap her. It was just a superstition, but she couldn't take any chances. She'd learnt that the hard way.

But this wasn't a bad day; this would be a good day- she'd make sure of it. She entered her building, running her knuckle along the radiator as she walked towards her office. It made a pleasing sound that rose in pitch when she reached the end. One of her rituals, but a fun one.

Jacquie was already in the galley kitchen, adding sugar to the first of the many strong coffees she required to make it through the day. Laura called a greeting to her friend, as she pulled the headphones from her ears. Jacquie shuffled out into the corridor and leant on the door frame for support.

"Morning, chickie. You're looking perky." She tucked a stray strand of red hair behind her ear and stifled a yawn. "I'm not up to full caffeine capacity yet- only got four hours sleep last night."

Laura grinned. Jacquie was the closest person she had to a best friend now, and she enjoyed living vicariously through her escapades. She was easy to chat to, although Laura kept their conversations light. It wouldn't do to share too much, to let anyone know.

"Clubbing on a school night? Tut tut," she teased. Jacquie was eight years younger than her, and contentedly single. Sometimes Laura envied her. She'd been content once too.

"It was awesome. Wild!" she laughed, before fixing her gaze on Laura. "You should come out one time, seriously."

Laura laughed nervously. "I'm too old."

Jacquie blew a raspberry in response to that. "Old-schmold. You might be nearly thirty but you're not dead yet. Come out for a quick drink after work- start the weekend off right. You'd enjoy it."

Laura didn't doubt she would. It had been so long since she'd had a night out anywhere, let alone without Adam. She chewed her lip; he wouldn't let her, so there was no point in asking him.

"It's a bit difficult at the moment…"

Jacquie snorted. "That pig. He keeps you on a tight leash, doesn't he?" Her tone was playful, but Laura felt the scorn in the words. She bristled defensively; Jacquie might be right, but it was none of her business. She didn't understand.

"I'd better get on. Thanks anyway." Laura turned away and entered her small office, closing the door on the conversation.

She hung her coat and scarf on the peg fixed to the back of the door and sat down in her chair. It squeaked grumpily as she shifted her weight to lean down and switch on the computer. Fridays were always busy, with everyone wanting things wrapped up before the weekend, but the Friday before a Bank Holiday was busier than usual. Then she had the long weekend to endure... three whole days with Adam and the chip on his shoulder.

She needed to do something about him.

Jacquie's words replayed themselves in her mind like a stuck record, and Laura shook her head to shake them out. It was important that she focus this morning; she couldn't work through lunch as she often did. Not today. She touched the wooden desk to reassure herself. Today was going to be a good day.

Laura spent the morning immersed in typing letters and checking emails. She paused only to tick off items on her to-do list, smiling smugly as the made progress with it, or answer the phone. Twice, she had to leap across the room to answer before the fifth ring, but she made it both times. Things were going her way.

She was pleased about this. It was important that she did everything right today. She smiled to herself, picturing the dress she was going to buy in her lunch break. She'd been waiting all week for the sale to begin, had gone without in order to save the money to buy it. It wasn't expensive- not by her previous standards- but it was a luxury she couldn't afford nowadays. It would be worth it though. Whenever she was sure no one was looking, she hugged herself in excitement.

As soon as the clock showed twelve o'clock, Laura threw down her pen and rushed to gather her things. She wrapped up warmly and headed for the town centre, shouting a quick goodbye to Jacquie as she left. Adam didn't know she was going to buy the dress today but, remembering Jacquie's words, Laura mentally stuck her tongue out at him. It was *her* money. She pulled her scarf up over her nose to hide the guilty flush of colour in her cheeks and thrust her hands deep into her pockets. The wind was nippy for the time of year, but it blew a white feather up in the air which landed at her feet, so she didn't mind. That meant angels were watching. This was good.

The heater over the shop door made her loosen the top buttons on her coat- only three though, as four would never do. The shop assistant glanced up and smiled at her in recognition as she served another customer. Laura had been in every day this week to check on her dress, waiting impatiently for the sale so she could afford it.

Laura slid the hangers along the metal rail, working her way through systematically, counting them just to be sure. She found two dresses in her size, but only in green. That would never do. Green was unlucky. She checked the others but they were either too big or too small. It dawned on her that she may have waited too long; she'd missed her chance- the dress had gone.

She searched through the hangers again, trying to be methodical, calm, pushing the panic away. She'd wanted this so much! She never spent money on herself! Didn't she deserve this one thing? After two more thorough hunts, she let her hands drop to her sides, her whole body deflated with confusion and defeat. Despite her efforts, it wasn't meant to be. Disappointed, she was about to leave when she spotted an electric-blue flash jumbled in with some beige cardigans.

She raced over and snatched it out. It was her dress, and in her size! This was good- in fact, better; it was a Sign. All her rituals had paid off today. She floated past the changing rooms and over to the till, her soon-to-be purchase held high in pride. The shop assistant scanned the dress and smiled at her.

"It must be your lucky day," she said. "This is in the sale." Laura smiled smugly. It was more than luck. "Would you like to try it on before you buy it?"

"No, thank you." She didn't like changing rooms: they had mirrors on three sides. She didn't like being trapped between mirrors.

"Well, it's in the sale, so you won't be able to return it if it doesn't fit- only if it's faulty."

"That's ok." She knew it would be ok. She tapped her foot and counted silently while she watched the shop assistant press buttons on the till.

"That'll be thirteen pounds exactly, please."

Laura stiffened. *Thirteen* pounds? She recovered and opened her purse, fumbling through it, trying to cover her tracks. The shop assistant waited patiently.

"Oh- I'm so sorry. I seem to have left my cards at home," Laura lied, as smoothly as she could manage, closing her purse on the crisp twenty pound note that waited there. The shop assistant pursed her lips. She obviously thought she was a time-waster.

"Would you like us to keep it back for you?" she asked, a hint of exasperation showing in her voice.

"No, no- I couldn't ask you to do that." Laura's cheeks flushed. The shop assistant eyed her coolly, raising one eyebrow slightly. She took the dress and hung it behind the counter without a word. Stuttering apologies, Laura left the shop, her face burrowed deep into her scarf.

What had gone wrong? She had done everything right today; she'd been so careful. Her brow furrowed into a frown as she mentally retraced her steps. *Pavement cracks, magpie, black cat, ladder...* No, she couldn't pinpoint where she'd made a mistake. She sighed. Maybe it just wasn't meant to be.

Laura returned to her office, twenty minutes early and downhearted. She avoided Jacquie's quizzical look, sliding straight into her chair and picking up the file she'd thrown to one side forty minutes previously. She worked through the remaining tasks on her list without enthusiasm, going through the motions as well as she could manage. Jobs were ticked off, emails responded to and phone calls answered, until she gradually felt that she was in control of herself again. It was a shame about the dress, but she'd coped with disappointment before; she'd survive. She filed the last batch of paperwork, leaned back in her chair and stretched her arms high above her head, allowing herself a small smile. *All done.*

"You staying here all night, Laura?" Jacquie poked her head around the door, her coat already on. Laura looked up quickly at the clock. It was already ten minutes past her finishing time. She leapt to her feet in a panic- she couldn't be late again; he'd be furious!

"No, I'm going now- I got caught up in what I was doing- I didn't realise the time." She stumbled over the words, feeling pressure constricting her throat. Jacquie watched as Laura hurriedly slipped her arms into her coat, picked up her handbag, dropped it, and picked it up again. She folded her arms and leaned against the door frame, a concerned frown puckering her brows.

"Calm down," she ordered. "It's not the end of the world

if he has his dinner a bit late tonight." She stepped to one side as Laura rushed past and out into the corridor, her coat unbuttoned and her scarf flapping loose. Laura heard Jacquie calling after her as she opened the door and ran out into the darkening evening.

"You shouldn't be so scared of him!"

Those workmen were there for once, waiting to catch her out. She checked the road before stepping out to avoid the ladder; she didn't trust her luck at the moment. She wanted to kick it, but the burly men would have seen and thought she was crazy. She cursed under her breath instead, at the stupid men and the stupid ladder and the stupid dress.

She'd been so careful. She puzzled over it as she ran, hopping between the paving slabs and pulling her scarf over her ears.

"Why *thirteen*?" she muttered, as she jogged past the police station. "Why that number?" She must have miscalculated the discount somehow, or else they'd discounted it further than they'd advertised. She shuddered. Just thinking about that number made her feel uncomfortable. It was the unluckiest number that existed; even so-called "normal" people were afraid of it. There was no question of her going back to buy it, not for- not for that number.

The uncomfortable feeling in her chest swelled as she stewed on the injustice of it all. If only she'd bought it last week, when she'd first seen it. If only she'd had the money. If only Adam would just-

A rare blaze of anger swept through her. This was Adam's fault. *Drunken layabout*, she seethed silently. *Parasite*. How she hated him. She tried so hard to make everything right, spent her whole day counting, checking, touching, avoiding- every ritual and superstition conceived to ward off the badness- and still he managed to ruin it.

She must do something about him.

She slowed to a walking pace at the corner, to allow her breathing to return to normal. She couldn't go home in this state. It wouldn't do. The street lamps winked on, their soft yellow light buzzing above her head. Normally, this would be good, but tonight she didn't think it would be enough. She counted red cars to distract herself from the growing unease as she turned off the road and onto her street. Her legs, unused to running so far, felt unsteady beneath her as she neared her house, avoiding drains, walking to the very inside of the pavement to keep as far away from them as she could. By the time she reached the gate, she was at least in control of her mind again, the bad thoughts subdued and replaced by anxiety. She was late.

She pushed the gate open cautiously, searching the lit windows for any movement or warning. All was quiet. Maybe he wasn't in. She checked her watch. Her sprint had caught up some time; she was only a few minutes later than normal. Maybe he wouldn't notice. She paused at her front door, mentally testing her composure. She could handle this.

From the hallway, she could hear gunfire coming from the living room. So he was home then. She slipped off her shoes and placed them neatly on the shoe rack, stooping to pick up Adam's trainers and tidy them away. She shrugged out of her coat and hung it, with her scarf, on the peg by the door. At the sound of his voice, low and ominous, she froze, hand still outstretched.

"You're late."

His words were thick with disapproval. Laura gulped.

"Had a lot to do today. Bank holiday and all that." She hated how apologetic she sounded, so weak and placating. She hadn't always been like that. Bracing herself, she

STRANGE IDEAS: DEATH, DESTINY AND DECISIONS

smoothed her hair and stepped into the living room.

Adam was sprawled across the sofa, the Xbox controller in his hands, debris from his day strewn around him. He was dressed, which was something, she supposed.

"Yeah, I forgot- your job is *so* important." She should be used to the sarcasm by now, but it still hurt her every time. Adam aimed his sights and fired, his fingers working the controls expertly, his eyes never leaving the screen. "What's for dinner? I'm starving."

Looking around at the crisp packets, mugs and plates that circled him, Laura doubted that statement. Her own stomach growled, reminding her that she'd skipped lunch today.

"Yeah, me too," she answered with false brightness. "I'll get something organised." She collected the mugs and plates, balancing them against her body as she went to the kitchen.

The breakfast things were where she had left them that morning, in the sink. She stacked the new additions by the side. She'd have to wash up before she could begin preparing dinner. Anger simmered again and she gnawed on her lip as she hurriedly swept up some salt that had been spilled, probably over the microwave chips he insisted on eating. All that unhealthy food; he'd give himself a heart attack one day. Throwing the salt quickly over her left shoulder, she blinked away the tantalising image of Adam, sprawled on the floor, clutching his chest. She shouldn't think bad things.

Adam had made himself lunch at home today: a bacon sandwich, judging from the empty wrapper on top of the cooker and the butter left out, a knife stabbed through the centre like a ghoulish table decoration. At least he hadn't been to the pub again; it was always worse when he'd spent the afternoon drinking. She filled the sink with water and grabbed a cloth to wipe up the ketchup that was smeared on the side.

Adam shuffled in behind her and watched in silence as she wiped, tidied, cleaned. He sniffed, and to Laura's heightened senses, even that small sound grated.

"How long are you going to be? I said I was starving."

Laura gripped the counter and fought the urge to scream. The kitchen light flickered and hummed, as if she sucked its energy for the strength to compose herself.

"Not long. I just need to straighten things up in here first." She kept her voice level and her back to him as she rinsed the cloth, pushing the anger down until it hardened into a ball in the pit of her stomach. It throbbed there, ticking like a bomb.

"If you were home on time for once, I wouldn't have to wait."

Laura gritted her teeth and ignored him, plunging her hands into the bubbles. Her fingers closed around the butter knife and she shut her eyes, imagining the look on his face if she were to suddenly spin around and thrust it into his chest. Her eyes shot open as the lights flickered again. She shouldn't think bad things. She let go of the knife and picked up a glass, pushing the cloth inside to scrub out the residue from the bottom.

"I couldn't help it, Adam. We were busy today. It was only a few minutes." She was less successful in controlling her tone this time; Adam detected the strain and pounced upon it.

"Why are you getting stroppy with me? You're the one who was late." In the kitchen window, she saw his reflection straighten from a slouch, his shoulders squaring up and his chest puffing out. *Here it comes...*

"I'm not getting stroppy; I'm just saying-"

He moved so fast that his reflection blurred. The slap cracked against the back of her head, throwing her forward.

STRANGE IDEAS: DEATH, DESTINY AND DECISIONS

The glass she was holding slipped from her hand and shattered against the draining board.

"You stupid cow! Look what you did!" Another slap, across her hunched shoulders this time. "Clean that up- and don't ever answer me back."

Hatred filled Laura's heart, black and poisonous, and she spun on her heels, pushed past him and ran into the hallway. She needed to get away from him, before something bad happened. She sprinted up the stairs, taking them two at a time, slammed the bedroom door and threw herself onto the bed, face down. *Don't- please, don't...*

His footsteps shook the house as he thundered up after her. Laura rolled over and sprang to her feet. She leapt for the door but was too late; Adam burst through it, his face puce and his cold eyes glinting evilly. A hint of a smirk danced on his lips; he had been waiting for this for days.

"Adam- don't," she warned, holding out her hands like they could fend him off. He took a step forward, careful to still block the doorway.

"Or what? You'll put a curse on me, you freak?" He laughed contemptuously. "You're crazy, you know that?" He took another bold step forward. Laura backed away, until her legs came up against the base of the bed.

"I'm warning you! You know what happens!" She shuffled sideways, away from him.

He paused, but only to laugh again.

"You really are messed up, aren't you? I don't know why I even bother with you." He shook his head slowly, looking her up and down with a pitying stare. Laura held her breath; this could go either way now. She tried once more.

"Remember last time?"

Something in her words made Adam pause- just for a second, but it was enough. He stuck his chin out, but seemed to be considering his options. She could almost see the thoughts lumbering around his stupid, Neanderthal head.

Finally, his lips curled in a sneer. "You're not even worth it, you freak." He stepped backwards, keeping her in view until he reached the door. She heard him thump down the stairs, then there was quiet for a few seconds before the front door slammed.

Laura exhaled slowly, closing her eyes and letting her head fall back. She sat down on the edge of the bed and sobbed, racking gasps that left her breathless. When she had washed out her sadness, she lay down and cried tears of frustration and anger instead. When her eyes were finally dry, she remained there, thinking, remembering.

He didn't get it. He never had. She spent her whole day counting, checking, touching, avoiding- because, if she didn't, bad things happened. The only reason he'd lasted so long in that job was because she'd kept him there, with her rituals and superstitions.

The argument they'd had, the one where she had stood her ground, had cost him his job. He didn't understand. He'd raised his fist to her and she had stopped protecting him, had let the bad thoughts take over until they spilled out of her mouth and poisoned the air. The universe had listened, and Adam had been punished. He didn't get it. He needed her- much more than she needed him. She could protect herself.

She lifted her hand to the back of her head; her skull was tender where he had hit her. Her heart hardened like the bone under her fingers. He wasn't going to do that again. She'd spent too many years appeasing, placating, *protecting* him because of her guilt over what she'd done. But he'd gone too far now.

Things were going to be very different from now on.

Feeling energised, Laura pulled herself off the bed and

went back downstairs. She cleaned up the mess Adam had left, knowing that she wouldn't sleep until everything was put back in the right place and all trace of him had been removed. She cleared up the broken glass in the kitchen and finished the washing up, smiling as she rinsed the butter knife, remembering that brief feeling of power as she'd held it hidden under the water; she knew what needed to be done now.

As she was drying her hands, her phone beeped. A message. She hoped it wasn't Adam, trying to apologise. It was too late for that; she'd made up her mind. Laura threw the towel in the washing machine and pulled the phone from her bag to read the message.

U ok? Was he cross? Worried so TMB xxx

Laura smiled down at the screen. Jacquie was kind, and more intuitive than she'd given her credit for. Maybe, once things were different, she could become a real friend. Laura hadn't had a real friend in years; Adam hadn't liked her making new friends that took her away from him. She typed her reply quickly.

I'm ok. Will text tomorrow xxx

Tomorrow it would be different. She switched her phone off and climbed the stairs to bed. She couldn't wait for tomorrow to arrive.

She undressed and burrowed under the covers, setting her alarm even though tomorrow was Saturday. As she drifted off to sleep, she let every bad thought she'd ever had about him fill her mind, colouring her dreams with a palette of blood and dirt. Tomorrow would be different- she'd make sure of it.

Laura awoke with a clear head and a secret smile on her lips. She rolled over to look at her alarm clock; the harsh green numbers declared that it was seven o'clock. Adam lay beside her, half-dressed and probably hung-over. She hadn't woken when he'd come home last night, hadn't stirred as he'd climbed into their bed. Her dreams had kept her too busy. She hit the snooze button and lay back, her arms stretched above her head like a sun-basking cat. She waited.

When the alarm sounded again, six hours and sixty-six minutes past midnight, she leaned over lazily to switch it off, letting the blaring din rip through the early-morning peace for a few more unnecessary seconds. Adam groaned and pulled the duvet over his head, muttering incomprehensible insults from within his disturbed dreams. She grinned spitefully and pulled back the duvet before sliding her feet into her slippers: *left* foot first, then the right.

In the bathroom, she hummed a tune as she brushed her teeth to distract herself from the urge to count. The early morning sun streamed through the windows, illuminating her face and creating a sparkle in her eyes. She grinned at herself in the mirror. Today was going to be a *good* day. She left the towel crooked, and continued her song as she skipped back to the bedroom to dress.

She needed something special to wear today. She knelt down and rummaged in the bottom of the wardrobe until she found the pale cream box with a lemon-yellow bow. Resting on her haunches, she untied the ribbon and removed the lid. Inside lay the blue garter she had worn on her wedding day. It was supposed to be lucky, something blue, but the lace had scratched her skin and given her a rash. She'd hated it. It wasn't a good start to married life. Throwing the box and lid back into the wardrobe, she stood up to choose her outfit.

She ignored the right-hand side of her wardrobe, seeking something from the left-hand side: something she did not wear very often. Memories tingled in her fingertips as she slid each hanger across the rail until she found the perfect outfit.

STRANGE IDEAS: DEATH, DESTINY AND DECISIONS

She hummed happily as she slid the garter onto her wrist and lifted off a hanger. A black dress, simple, modest, sombre. She only wore it for funerals. Those were bad days. It was perfect. She slipped it over her head and pulled up the zip, smoothing the material over her hips. She poked her left leg through the garter and pulled it up to above her knee, ignoring the itchy lace which scratched like a hair shirt.

Penance for my sins.

She inspected herself in the full-length mirror hanging on the bedroom wall and fought the urge to giggle like a naughty school-girl. She looked ridiculous, in her funeral-dress and bed-hair, the shape of the garter visible beneath the black material clinging to her thighs. Satisfied, she turned around to gaze down on the wrong side of the bed and the still-sleeping figure. He snored, mouth lolling open, and did not wake. His face was blank, oblivious to the countdown.

She smiled and closed the bedroom door quietly before descending the stairs, left foot first, and making her way to the kitchen.

She pulled up the blinds to let the sunshine flood in and prepared her breakfast. The street outside was still and empty: a stage awaiting its cast. She boiled the kettle and poured it over the teabag, being sure to stir the spoon anti-clockwise. As she poured in the milk, she deliberately splashed some on the worktop. *Let the fairies have it*, she thought, grinning wickedly.

After a moment's deliberation, she pulled open a cupboard door and reached for the salt cellar, tipping it upside down and watching the white grains fall like snow onto the milk, where they dissolved to form a sticky mess. No chance of picking the grains up now.

Not satisfied with that, she selected a knife from the

drawer and turned, letting it fall from her fingers and drop to the floor. It clattered loudly, each jarring peal sending a thrilling shock through her body. Bending carefully, so as not to dislodge the garter, she picked up the knife herself. She stood and held it aloft, like a villain caught red-handed and unrepentant, before throwing it into the sink.

Sipping her tea in the dining room, looking out into the back garden with its overgrown shrubs and mouldy pots, her eyes flitted from tree to tree, searching. At last, she saw one. She fixed her gaze on the black and white bird, head steady, no hint of a nod. It looked back at her, and she imagined it asked her a question.

Are you sure?

"Yes," she said aloud, her head still and her heart pounding. She would not nod a reply. The magpie flew away. She drained her mug and pulled on her boots and coat, grabbing her handbag from the newel post. She marched down the garden path out onto the pavement.

The early morning air seemed scented with promise, the breeze dancing round her playfully until she became light-headed with the joy of it. She was glad it was too early for many people to be up and about- what would the neighbours think of her, dancing down the street and stepping on every crack she could see?

She followed her usual route to work. As she rounded the corner, she exhaled in relief at the sight of the previously-dreaded scaffolding. The burly workmen were there, for once, even though it was Saturday and not yet eight o'clock, dismantling the platforms and supports. *Not yet!* She needed it! She quickened her pace, and one of them looked up at the sound of her footsteps, moving aside to let her pass. She smiled brightly at him, her heart singing with laughter and boldness as she squeezed by him and walked under the ladder propped up against the wall.

"That's bad luck, you know," he called after her as she danced away.

She twirled to call back, "I know," without stopping her dance.

She was breathless with exhilaration by the time she reached the shop. It wasn't open yet; she was far too early. She leaned up against the glass and shielded her eyes so she could peer through at the racks of clothes set neatly on runner rails. A snicker slipped through her lips and her teeth reflected back at her as she burst out into a wide smile. What she was going to do was so *wrong* that it felt naughty, like bunking off school or telling lies. The old, cautious part of her trembled at the next part of her plan. The new, dangerous part of her couldn't wait.

She backed away from the window, laughing again at her reflection, before twirling further down the high street and flopping onto a bench. What now? *Oh, yes.*

She pulled her phone from her bag and dialled Jacquie's number. Straight to answerphone. Jacquie was probably still in bed- whose, she couldn't guess.

"Hi, Jacquie?" Laura heard her voice, high and unnatural, as she spoke into the phone. "It's Laura. I've been thinking, and I've decided I would like very much to come out with you sometime. In fact, how about tonight?" Laura searched through her memory for a bar that Jacquie had mentioned before. "Let's say, The Peacock? Eight o'clock?"

She looked down the high street; two women in upmarket-casual uniforms were pulling up the shutters over the doors of the shop. "I've bought a new dress especially." She giggled, feeling giddy with nerves. "I'll see you there." She disconnected the call and shoved her phone back into her bag.

She sat for a while, swinging her legs and enjoying the sunshine, until she saw the shop doors open. Bouncing from the bench, she scooped up her bag and hurried along to buy her dress.

The heater over the door blew her hair as she walked in, mussing it up so it looked even worse than when she had left the house. Uncaring, Laura marched straight over to the rack of dresses and pulled out a green one in her size. She held it up against herself, stroking the fabric and plucking up the courage to go through with what she'd planned.

The shop assistant eyed her suspiciously. Laura didn't blame her; it was a different woman to yesterday, one she didn't know, and she had to admit that she probably looked a little scatty right now.

She took a deep breath and walked up to the shop assistant.

"Good morning," Laura said brightly. "I'd like to try this on, please."

"Certainly," the woman smiled, relaxing slightly. "The changing rooms are this way." She gestured to a door next to the till that lead to a corridor of changing rooms.

"Thank you." Laura kept smiling as she turned and headed towards them.

She hovered in the threshold of the third changing room. Her reflection in the mirror facing her stared back, face pale and cheeks flushed. She couldn't believe she was about to do this. Laura held her breath, closed her eyes, and stepped forward. There. She was surrounded on three sides by mirrors. This was seriously bad luck. She kept her eyes closed while she tested the feeling. It didn't feel strange at all, not really. She peeked out from beneath her eyelashes at the reflection in front of her. Her reflection peeked back, the half-wink looking cheeky. Laura laughed and opened her eyes fully, spinning on her toes to draw the heavy crimson curtain closed.

She wriggled out of her funeral-dress and slipped the emerald-green one over her head. Pulling up the zip, she gazed at the woman in the mirror. Her skin seemed smoother, creamy against the bold colour of the dress. Her cheeks held a becoming blush of colour, and her eyes shone richly, complementing the tones of the material. Green suited her. Who'd have guessed?

She changed back into her black dress and left the changing room, carrying the green one in front of her like a flag. It really was a very pretty green, she decided, like grass in the summer. She took her place to pay.

"It must be your lucky day," the shop assistant said. "This is in the sale." Laura smiled knowingly and pulled out her twenty pound note. The woman folded the dress and placed it in a bag. "Thirteen pounds, please."

If Laura's fingers trembled slightly as she handed over the money, only Laura noticed it. The shop assistant handed her back her change and her new purchase.

"Thank you," Laura said, before she could change her mind.

"My pleasure. Enjoy your day."

"Oh, I will."

Laura hugged the bag to her as she walked along the road. She'd done it! Delicious, unfamiliar feelings swept over her as she danced down the road towards home. Ever since she'd woken up, she had been doing things wrong, messing up her rituals, ignoring her superstitious instinct. She felt wanton, wild, on top of the world. She couldn't wait for tonight. She wondered if anything had happened to Adam yet.

She imagined him slipping in the shower, cracking his

head and falling unconscious to drown in a half-inch of water. Her mind rebelled automatically against the image, her in-built censor wanting to push the bad thought away; she held onto to it, stubbornly. Today was different.

When she got home, she ran straight upstairs to hang her dress up before it creased. The bathroom was empty of corpses, to her disappointment. Adam was still in bed. He lifted his head from the pillow to squint at her, unrepentant and tetchy.

"What's that?" he asked.

"A dress." Her back tensed automatically, from years of being cautious, before she remembered that today was different. She pulled an empty hanger from the wardrobe and hung the dress on it.

"Where from?"

"A shop." *What a stupid question to ask*. Laura imagined him dressed as a village idiot, and mentally put him in the stocks; instead, rather than rotten fruit, she was going to throw bricks and sharp things at him, every time he spoke.

Adam eyed her warily, more awake now and sensing the change in her mood. It wasn't just the strange way she was dressed. It was the way she flounced in, the way she spoke to him. She wasn't normally like this. He didn't like it.

"Why are you wasting money on a dress? It's not like you go anywhere."

Laura threw an imaginary rock. "Ah, but you see Adam," she said, wagging a finger at him. "That's all going to change from now on. I'm going out tonight."

"Tonight?" his mouth hung open, stupidly. Laura laughed as she imagined his teeth falling out. Adam took a breath, ready to retort, but Laura shot him a look, so cold, so venomous, that he closed his mouth and shrank back into the safety of the mattress.

"Yes, tonight," she said firmly. "I'm going clubbing with Jacquie."

Adam harrumphed but didn't argue. He didn't know this Laura. He needed to retreat, regroup, rethink his attack. He hid his head under the covers to shield his eyes from the light and the woman he didn't recognise.

Laura changed into her scruffy jogging bottoms and pulled an old jumper over her head. Buoyed up by his silence and her own exhilaration, she continued. "I'm going to do some gardening today, so you'll need to sort your own breakfast out. I shan't have time to make you lunch either. And I expect I'll be too busy for dinner too."

Before he could respond, she turned on her heel and scampered down the stairs, running from his disapproval. She'd told him! And this was just the start!

Out in the garden she quickly got to work. First, she scrubbed the pots and planters, then she weeded the borders, before finally trimming the rose bush that trailed across the fence and over the other side. She pulled the thorny stems free, their sharp points stabbing like daggers against her fingers. Every now and then, when she looked up, she caught sight of Adam, watching her from the house with a thoughtful expression on his face. She ignored him; he'd be gone soon.

The sun rose higher into the sky as she worked, its warmth feeling good on her skin as she turned her face up to greet it: energising her, feeding her, filling the old greyness inside with butter-yellow happiness. She dragged what she'd cleared down to the end of the garden and piled it up, ready for a bonfire. She imagined dragging Adam down there next, tossing him on top of the prickly branches before dropping a match and watching him roast. Her bad thoughts were getting stronger now, more vivid, more powerful. She even thought she could hear him scream this time, as the flames licked and devoured his lazy body.

She felt someone's eyes on her and, out of habit, she started guiltily- but the eyes weren't Adam's. He'd given up glaring out of the window hours ago as it was clearly having no effect on her. He'd probably sought refuge in the pub by now. Good. She hoped they'd serve him line cleaner by mistake.

She looked around the garden, curious as to who was watching. Two green eyes studied her from the remains of the rose bush by the fence- a cat, black as midnight. For a second, Laura's heart skipped a beat and she straightened up, ready to run back inside the house. Old habits died hard. She took a moment to compose herself, and then called the cat towards her. It examined her from a safe distance, interested but not tempted. She'd have to make the first move. She took a small step forward; she didn't want to frighten it away. It slid out of the bush, stretched and strolled nonchalantly towards her.

"Here, puss," she crooned, holding her hand out, her fingernails crusted with earth. "Good kitty." The cat let her touch his face and run her hand down his side. He was soft, like the hair on a baby's head. He leaned against her hand, purring contently. She stepped back, still cooing, and he moved forward to rub himself against her legs. She laughed, delighted to break another rule- and in her own garden- and stepped back again, letting the cat cross her path before she walked forward.

They played that game for a few minutes; each time the black cat crossed her path her spine tingled with the thrill of it. She quite liked this cat; he seemed friendly. But she still would prefer a dog. Chocolate-brown eyes drifted into her mind; tiny pink pads and a black button nose.

STRANGE IDEAS: DEATH, DESTINY AND DECISIONS

Soon.

"You won't be able to visit much, puss," she whispered to the cat. "Not when I get my dog."

She waved the cat goodbye and went inside to clean herself up and make something to eat before her evening's adventure. The house was empty and silent. Good. She hoped Adam was drinking himself senseless, and that he wouldn't come back. Closing her eyes, she imagined him being hit by a car as he stumbled home from the pub, and shivered with delight. Bad thoughts made bad things happen. Adam would learn that the hard way. It wouldn't be long now. She poured herself a glass of wine and checked her phone.

You're on! The message read. *See you there at 8 xxx*

Laura clapped her hands before draining her glass. Tonight was going to be *fun*.

The bar was already crowded when Laura arrived. Her blonde hair was pinned up on top of her head, soft tendrils bouncing in gentle waves besides the lashings of mascara she had applied to her eyelashes. Her skin gleamed thanks to the lavish application of her favourite body lotion; it was the expensive stuff, the bottle she'd got for Christmas and was saving for a special occasion. Today *was* special. She was making sure of it. She'd also treated herself to a taxi; her heels were meant to be admired, not walked in. She scanned the room for a flash of red curls, but saw none. She was a little early, but she'd been too twitchy to wait.

Taking a deep breath, she walked over to the bar, acutely aware of the heads that turned and the eyes that followed her steps. She flushed, flattered but unused to the attention. Two men, in smart shirts and jeans, parted to make way for her at the bar.

"Thank you," she smiled. Funny how people treated her differently in this dress; maybe they could tell.

The barman skipped a few customers to serve her first. Laura was flustered for a moment; what did people drink nowadays? She guessed and asked for a cocktail, and he reeled off a list of mysterious names that sounded to her like a foreign language.

"...Black Velvet, Singapore Sling, Bloody Mary, Long Island Iced Tea, Screwdriver, Black Russian, Grasshopper, Death in the Afternoon-"

Laura held up her hand to stop him.

"Wait, what was that last one again?"

"Death in the Afternoon?"

"Yes." She liked the sound of that one. "What's in it?"

"Absinthe and champagne. It's quite strong."

Champagne. Champagne for a celebration. It was a Sign. She pulled out her purse.

"I'll have two."

The barman nodded and turned away to mix her order. Laura leant on the bar and checked her hair in the mirror behind the exotically-coloured bottles on display. Her foot tapped in time to the beat of Blondie's "Rapture"- one of her favourites, though she'd not heard it in years. Not since the cheesy 80s disco nights she used to go to, back at University.

So much time wasted since those days.

"Two drinks? You must be tougher than you look."

Laura turned her head to her left. One of the men who had made way for her earlier was now admiring her openly. Laura smiled, but only politely; she didn't want to encourage him.

"I'm meeting a friend."

"Boyfriend? Husband?" He eyed her hand, looking for a ring. She wasn't wearing one. It was on the dresser back home, where she'd left it.

"Just a friend."

"Right." He turned on the charm. "So, you must be new around here. I would have remembered your face otherwise."

"And I certainly remember yours, Pete." Jacquie slid in between them, planting herself firmly in the middle. "Go tell some other sap about your ex-wife and your commitment issues." She picked up the fizzing glass that the barman placed on the bar and turned her back on an embarrassed Pete. "We're celebrating my good friend's night of freedom."

Laura picked up the other glass and knocked it against Jacquie's.

"We certainly are."

Many hours, too many drinks and much laughter later, Laura excused herself to visit the ladies. She'd decided that drinking cocktails in noisy bars was something she could get used to, but her bladder was protesting and she knew she wouldn't last another round of drinks.

Jacquie was holding court with a group of friends who'd joined them earlier in the evening. Laura could hear their cackles as she wobbled her way through the crowd towards the toilets. They were a nice mix, accepting her immediately on the strength of Jacquie's recommendation, and they certainly were funny. Laura couldn't remember the last time she'd laughed so hard.

She washed her hands and dried them quickly, eager to rejoin her new friends. She reapplied her lipstick in the mirror and checked she had none on her teeth, grinning tipsily at her reflection. She looked so different; she *felt* so different. Gone was the grey, downtrodden shell of herself, approaching middle age and sleep-walking through life. She'd been replaced by a bright young woman in her prime, who had friends, opportunities- a future to look forward to. She twirled slowly to admire her new dress from every angle, the stylish lighting making it gleam like a jewel. It was as gorgeous as she'd dreamt, although, of course, she never would have imagined herself wearing the green version. She giggled and blew herself a kiss in the mirror before she picked up her handbag and unlocked the door.

As she walked back out into the main room, her good mood evaporated and her heart sank. Adam was here. He could barely stand, holding onto the bar and arguing with the barman who had refused to serve him. Laura considered leaving out the back, running away, avoiding the scene, but the cocktails had given her courage and so she straightened her shoulders instead. She was tired of being afraid of him; she could handle this.

She pushed past drinkers to reach the bar; an empty circle surrounded Adam, as if the other customers sensed things were about to turn ugly and wanted to watch from a safe distance. She tapped him on the shoulder. He wheeled round, unsteady on his feet, mouth open ready to hurl abuse. His jaw dropped when he realised who she was.

"Wha' you doin' here?" he slurred, frowning, though through confusion or anger she wasn't sure.

"Adam, go home." She spoke quietly, calmly. She could handle this. The crowd held its breath, waiting to see what would happen now.

"You can' tell me wha' to do!" He turned fully to face her, using the bar to support himself. She took hold of his arm, meaning to lead him out of the bar and into a taxi. He knocked her hand away and spat on the floor at her feet. "You ge' away from me, you stupid- you freak!"

The crowd gasped and, from the corner of her eye, Laura saw Jacquie stand and start fighting her way over. She needed to end this- now.

"You're drunk. Go home." Her tone was firmer now; a sober man would have heard the menace and heeded the warning. "This is the last time I'm going to tell you."

Adam's voice was loud over the sudden hush in the room. "You don' tell me anything!" he bellowed, before lurching forward, his fist raised to strike her.

There was no saving him now, not even if she'd wanted to. She dodged the first swing and spun on her toes, darting back through the crowd who parted, too stunned to do anything else, to let her through. She raced to the toilets, aware of Adam's angry roar following her. For a drunk man, he moved fast.

She threw herself through the door and turned to push it shut, but she wasn't quick enough. Adam charged before she could close it, knocking her to the floor with the force of his entry. Laura scrambled to her feet, losing a shoe in the process, the tiles cold against her bare foot.

"I'm goin' to show you," he rambled, his blood-shot eyes wild. "Goin' show you what happens-"

He didn't get to finish his sentence.

Laura launched herself at him, anger giving her strength she didn't know she possessed, and he fell backwards against the sink, his head flinging back and cracking against the mirror with a sickening sound. Fragments of mirror slid from the wall and landed in the sink and on the floor in tinkling notes that echoed around the small room. There was moment of stunned silence before Adam groaned and righted himself, hand pressed against the back of his head. Blood dripped from between his fingers and onto the tiles. He stared incredulously at it. Laura held her breath, poised to make a dash for the exit.

"You- you little…" Adam seemed dazed; it had been a

hard blow. Laura sensed her chance. She edged towards the door, keeping her eyes locked on his.

Adam saw what she was doing and snatched up a shard of the broken mirror from the sink. He rushed at Laura, who ducked instinctively, curling her body into as small a target as possible. She didn't see what happened, only heard the skid of his shoes and the thud as his body hit the floor. She jumped up and backed away from him, ready to react to his next attempt.

There wasn't going to be one.

The fragment of broken mirror jutted out of Adam's chest, feeding a pool of blood which was spreading before her eyes. He tried to sit up, sucking in gurgling breaths and slicing his hands as he tugged at the sharp sliver, his shirt a crimson curtain of blood. As he'd fallen, he must have put his hands out to break his fall, only he'd fallen with his full weight onto the jagged shard instead. An accident.

Bad luck.

Except Laura knew better.

The weight of what she'd caused hit Laura like a physical blow. She dragged her eyes away from the wound and forced herself to look at Adam's face. Adam blinked, his blood-slicked hand outstretched to reach her, though whether in rage or remorse she'd never know.

She stood over him, unsure of her feelings now the moment had come. All day, she'd been wishing accidents on him, had deliberately encouraged the bad thoughts, wanting to be rid of him- but she hadn't thought it would be like this, not really. She didn't think she'd be there to see it happen. She knelt down and took his hand; his grip was weak, his strength fading as his life ebbed away on the floor of a ladies' toilet.

I loved him once.

STRANGE IDEAS: DEATH, DESTINY AND DECISIONS

The door moved as someone tried to push it open. What had felt like minutes had actually only been seconds. It had all happened so fast. Adam, or Adam's body as it was rapidly becoming, blocked the door. Voices outside shouted for the unknown pusher to move out of the way and seconds later Laura fell back as once more the door flew open, shoving Adam's body to the side of the room.

The barman fell into the room, took in the bloody scene and called over his shoulder.

"Phone an ambulance!"

Another barman, carrying a medical kit, squeezed into the now cramped room and knelt down by Adam. He rolled him onto his back and leant over, his ear against Adam's mouth. His eyes flicked up briefly from Adam's chest to Laura's face before he sat up and began unwrapping wads of bandages to press around the wound, avoiding her gaze as he worked.

Laura turned her head away, pulling her legs up and wrapping her arms around them. Outside, she could hear someone asking people to move out of the way and go back in the main bar, their voice sounding increasingly stern over the uproar. The barman, the one who'd made her cocktails, pulled the door almost closed, blocking any view in or out with his body.

"Laura? Laura!" She could hear Jacquie's voice over the row in the corridor. "Is she hurt? Did he-?" then an impatient "Get out of the way!"

The door opened fully and the barman was elbowed to one side by a determined Jacquie. She skidded over to where Laura sat, curled up in the corner by the hand-dryer, and dropped to her knees to envelope her in a hug.

"Oh my God, Laura!" She pulled back, using the sleeve of her top to wipe Laura's face. Laura was surprised to find she was crying; she didn't know at which point the tears had started to fall.

"Are you ok? What did he-?" Her words broke off as she spotted Adam's body, sprawled inelegantly on his back, eyes blank, the blood-smeared spike stabbed through the centre of his chest, visible despite the wadding the increasingly desperate barman was pressing down. She breathed in sharply. "Jesus…"

"It- it was an accident," Laura whimpered. "He was trying to-" She swallowed down the bile that was rising in her throat. "-and he slipped… he fell-" Jacquie cut her off.

"Don't. It's ok. We all saw him out there. There'll be dozens of witnesses to say he was drunk and tried to hurt you." She rubbed Laura's back, trying to soothe her. Over Jacquie's shoulder, Laura saw the barman nodding vigorously in agreement. Jacquie continued. "It's not your fault. He slipped, like you said. He shouldn't have been-" She looked around at the broken fragments, each one a deadly weapon in dangerous hands. She shuddered, and pulled Laura closer. "Well, it was an accident," she whispered. "Just bad luck."

"Yeah." Laura stared at the patterned wallpaper, her eyes glazed, and thought of the salt, the pavement cracks, the ladder. She remembered the dress, the black cat, the broken mirror. She knew what she'd caused.

She screwed up her fists as the memories and images and bad thoughts howled in her head, screaming in an echoing frenzy until she wanted to press her hands over her ears to block them out.

But she couldn't. They were inside her; she'd invited them in.

She knew what she'd caused. But no one else must ever know.

She smiled weakly up at Jacquie's face, full of concern and compassion for her friend. Laura nodded slightly, then again, more decisively. No one would ever know.

"Yes," she agreed. "Just bad luck."

LATE: A GHOSTLY TALE

The door hissed, a whisper that shimmered down the short corridor, and clicked shut with a sharp sound that was just on the edge of hearing. She was alone. Again. It wasn't the first time. She was often the last to leave, preferring to muster the effort to finish her marking at school rather than lug a bag of books home; they would only sit staring accusingly from the hallway until she dealt with them. But, as the silence fell around her like a cloak, part of her wished she was going home now too. It always felt so different here after everyone had gone.

The village school was tiny by most people's standards: two classrooms, a staff room and office, and a toilet block. All the rooms except one classroom branched off from a squat, rectangular corridor that multi-tasked as a cloakroom and led to the main entrance. The cheerful colours of the butterfly-themed display- primary in every sense- seemed false as darkness fell, like heavy make-up on a wizened face. Which in a way, she thought, it was.

The school was well over one hundred years old and, even though it had the necessary updates, didn't wear them happily. The interactive whiteboard, blank and silent since the children had left hours before, hung embarrassedly between two original chimney breasts. The fireplaces had been boxed in long ago, but the mantelpieces made it easy to visualise how they must once have looked. The windows, high and arched, let in light but not life- no distractions allowed here!

She listened to the car outside start up and watched the flash of headlights sweep a gentle glow past the tall windows before it drove away. Too late now.

She huffed resignedly and turned back to her books, her hair- strands of premature-grey contrasting with her natural brown tones- falling over her face as she bent to peer more closely at the sprawl on the page.

"Oh, Tom," she tutted. "How many times..?" She chewed the end of her green pen, thinking carefully how to phrase the correction.

A click, loud in the silence, broke her focus. Her head turned quickly towards the sound. Was that the main door? Sometimes it bounced and didn't catch as it shut. She knew she'd have to check: she was vulnerable here, alone, and the image of a shadowy prowler testing an unlocked door made her shiver. She pushed back her chair and walked hurriedly towards the main entrance.

The October blackness pressed against the windows and made the diminutive corridor feel like a submarine. As she tested the main door, rattling it sharply to check the catch, she half expected to see fish swimming past the glass panel. *Or maybe a face looming suddenly from the dark night.* As the thought, unwanted, popped into her head, she took an involuntary step back from the glass.

"Stop being stupid," she muttered, trying to disguise her fear with an impatient tone. "You'll only scare yourself." She rattled the door one more time and walked back to her classroom, being careful to keep her eyes lowered and away from the windows in the corridor.

"Right, where was I? Oh, yes- trying to be tactful..." She picked up her pen and wrote quickly and neatly at the bottom of the page. Shutting out the groans and creaks that are inevitable in any old building, she settled down to her task and was satisfied to see the previously intimidating pile whittled down to nothing.

"Awesome. Now that's done, I can get home."

She often spoke out loud to herself; it had become a habit. Living alone, with only her dogs, she had become used to talking to them as she went about her day, and a patter of external monologue was comforting even here. It made her feel less isolated. She considered it thinking aloud rather than talking to herself.

"And only crazy people talk to themselves," she murmured, smiling wryly as she stacked the marked books tidily, ready for tomorrow.

The click made her jump this time and she clutched the books to her chest, as if for protection, as she whirled to face the classroom door.

"Hello?" she called, hoping to hear the voice of the evening cleaner respond in greeting. Silence. And then- unmistakeably- another click.

The hairs on the back of her neck prickled as she quietly laid the books down on the table and moved silently closer to the door that led from her classroom out into the corridor. She inched around the doorframe and stared past the PE kits and forgotten lunchboxes at the main entrance door. It looked closed.

Rationally, she knew it was closed- hadn't she checked it herself? - but she couldn't shake the feeling that someone had just entered the building. Nor could she convince herself that the fresh waft of fragrant autumn air was purely her imagination. It hung there, almost tangible: the crisp coolness of almost-winter with an earthy taste.

Normally the changing of seasons was one of her favourite scents, but it was unwelcome here, where it stood out like a scream from the usual old-fruit-and-trainers combination found in most places where children's belongings congregate. She froze, listening carefully, ears straining for any further clue.

Nothing. Not even a hint at what had caused the mysterious click.

Scolding herself for her foolishness, she marched the short distance to the main door and rattled it vigorously. She let out a sigh of relief; she had not even been aware that she was holding her breath until she released it in a slow whoosh that seemed to take some of her tension with it.

"Spooked myself. That's obviously my cue to leave." She let go of the door handle and turned towards the staffroom. "Might as well make sure this end is all locked up."

The staffroom was a low-ceilinged modern extension to the original building. It housed the usual school paraphernalia: kettle, photocopier, cupboards full of outdated schemes of work that no-one ever seemed to throw away. Teachers were hoarders, guarding every potentially useful resource in case policy changed and it came back into fashion.

She checked the windows were locked, switched off all the appliances at the plugs, and was standing in the doorway just about to switch off the light when she saw it.

Or rather, she didn't see it. As she'd turned her head, she'd seen- she thought she'd seen- movement out of the corner of her eye. A shadow scampering quickly across the corridor-cloakroom and into Class 2- her classroom.

She stood as still as a statue, her body tensed, her mouth

dry, as her brain tried to make sense of it. Again her ears strained for any sound and her eyes searched the open doorway for any movement within the classroom. Seconds stretched into minutes, until her heart stopped pounding and returned to an almost normal pace. Still she could hear or see nothing unusual.

"Imagining things now," she whispered, unsure of why she had lowered her voice. "Just get your bag and go."

It took a few seconds to persuade her legs to move but, when they did, she strode purposefully into her classroom where she hurriedly switched off the computer and packed her diary and memory stick into her handbag. She made as much noise as she could, as if the loud commotion could scare away the monster her tired mind had created, or put a facade of normality on her desperate escape

With her bag tucked under her arm and her keys grasped tightly in her hand, she almost ran to the classroom door, closing it behind her as she switched off the light. She was nearly at the main door when the gaudy butterflies caught her eye and she remembered Class 1.

"Crap!"

Before leaving each night, the last member of staff on the premises needed to make sure the building was secure before locking up. This included checking both the classrooms and the other rooms. In her hurry to flee she'd abandoned her usual routine and so had almost forgotten to check Class 1.

She briefly contemplated just leaving anyway- most likely Ruth had checked everything there before she'd left earlier- but she knew that if anything happened overnight, she'd be to blame.

"With great power comes great responsibility," she sighed, trying to push down the sick feeling of dread. "Well, I'll just have to do it fast."

STRANGE IDEAS: DEATH, DESTINY AND DECISIONS

She turned, still clutching her handbag and keys, and tip-toed softly back to her classroom door.

Beyond the glass panel was inky darkness; it made her pause, her knuckles turning white where she gripped the handle of the door. Steeling herself, she turned it and reached inside, feeling along the wall for the light switch, her eyes closed so that she wouldn't see anything in the shadows. It seemed to take an age and panic bubbled in her stomach as she imagined her hand brushing against something unexpected. She fumbled for the switch along the cold painted brick wall, moving her hand lower, then higher, with a growing urgency that matched her increasing heartbeat. At last, her fingers found the switch and she opened her eyes as the fluorescent lights flickered indecisively.

There it was again. As each brief flash lit up the large classroom it revealed a dark figure, about four feet tall and oddly two-dimensional, with no defining features. It was standing at the door between the two classes.

She gasped and her stomach looped with terror. The light finished dithering and decided to stay. She blinked rapidly and the figure vanished, leaving only an image on the insides of her eyelids.

Horror washed over her like a bucket of ice. Her hand froze at the switch and her skin tingled in shock. What had she just seen? Was it real? Petrified, she stared at the spot where the figure had been and tried to think of a reasonable explanation. Her eyes playing tricks in the fluttering transition from dark to light? Her mind fooling her into seeing an intruder that she'd imagined? Or something else?

She realised she was panting, and made a conscious effort to breathe deeply and slowly. She didn't really feel like analysing it at this precise moment. Right now, she wanted to get out of there as fast as possible. But that meant heading towards the spot where she'd seen- whatever that thing was- and entering Class 1.

The urge to turn and run was overwhelming. Every instinct told her that something bad was waiting for her in the next room. She wished she had someone she could call, and her thumb rubbed the third finger of her left hand in an unconscious movement, feeling for the security of the wedding band that lay, discarded, in a jewellery box at home.

She hovered in the doorway, torn between reason and self-preservation, her heart thumping hard in her chest and the butterflies in her stomach flapping their wings frantically.

A car sped past outside, its stereo blaring, bringing her close to the real world for a few sweet seconds. The brief reminder shook her out of her inertia and she made up her mind. She would march into the room, check the doors and windows, and then march back and straight out of the main door, to the safety of her car. It would take thirty seconds, that's all. Then she would be free to drive home and have a good laugh with her friends about over-work and over-active imaginations.

Spotting her staple gun on top of the filing cabinet, she crossed the classroom quickly and picked it up. It felt good to have a weapon, of sorts, although the rational part of her brain did question its effectiveness against shadow people. She laid her bag and keys on a nearby table, never taking her eyes from Class 1's door.

Her legs trembled, but her resolve, if not her courage, was firm now and, with conscious effort, she stepped up to the door and turned the handle. She pushed the door open boldly, brandishing the staple gun like a cross between a pistol and a crucifix.

STRANGE IDEAS: DEATH, DESTINY AND DECISIONS

The classroom seemed darker than normal. Was that just her imagination? The pool of light from her own classroom barely illuminated the room in front of her, stopping at her feet as if it were too afraid to follow her in. The moon cast a muted glow from behind the blinds, but its light seemed to be swallowed by the blackness emanating from the corners of the room.

She stepped cautiously through the threshold, one hand wielding her make-shift weapon while the other held the heavy door open. The air tasted stale as it escaped past her.

She scanned the room nervously. Was that a figure crouched in the book corner? Or a discarded jumper, abandoned in the rush to race home in time for a game of football before tea? She hesitated, suddenly aware of how ridiculous she must look. A grown woman, armed with school stationery, reduced to a quivering wreck by a few bumps and shadows.

She lowered the staple gun and took a slow step forward, letting the door shut softly behind her.

Ten steps. That was all it would take to reach the door leading to the outside area. Ten steps, one push to check it was closed, and then she could leave.

It was clear from here that the windows were closed. The light switch was somewhere in the blackness off to her right; the door was just visible around the corner to her left. Ten steps. It would take more than ten steps to get to the light switch. She took a deep, steadying breath.

Sliding her feet carefully forward, so as not to trip in the darkness, she edged her way over to the door. *One step, two steps...* With every shuffle forwards, the pressure in her chest increased. *Three...* The short distance stretched endlessly. *Four, five-*

She was halfway there when panic-induced adrenalin

forced her to run the rest of the distance and almost throw herself at the door. It was firmly closed. She cursed under her breath. From behind her came a soft giggle.

She stiffened, unable to move, her body rigid with fright. The laughter came again, gleeful and child-like. She had heard that sort of laughter before, from the lips of a six year old as he pulled the wings from a butterfly he had trapped. Her heart stuttered. The air behind her seemed to change in consistency, growing thicker and closer. She closed her eyes and breathed deeply. This couldn't be happening.

Something cold touched her upper arm and she yelped at its icy temperature. It was like tendrils of sea-mist, caressing her skin and sliding smoothly down to her hand, where it wrapped around her fingers. They stood there for a moment, hands locked together, the touch insubstantial yet its grasp unbreakable.

It tugged insistently. She tried to resist, shaking her head mutely, but it pulled again. Eyes screwed tightly shut, she allowed herself to be turned so her back was against the outside door. She took another breath, and a whimper escaped her lips. The clammy grip tightened as she was led, helplessly, forwards into the centre of the classroom.

Another icy hand gripped her shoulder, and she was pulled down onto her knees, the staple gun clattering uselessly to the ground beside her. Now they were face to face.

She tried to breathe shallowly, not wanting to inhale the mist she imagined it to be made from. This close, it smelt of decaying leaves and wilting flowers, damp earth and dirty pebbles.

The second hand released her shoulder and took her empty hand, which tingled as the freezing fog wrapped itself around her fingers. She could feel chilled breath on her face;

it tasted sweet, like night-time rain. Her eyes were still tightly shut. She realised she did not want to see it, did not want its eyes to haunt her nightmares.

She was powerless: pinned like a butterfly on a mounting board, a motionless addition to a collection. She felt, rather than saw, its eyes roaming over her face. She guessed, rather than knew, that it was searching for something in her features. What was it searching for? What did she have that it wanted?

Her eyes pricked with tears but she fought the urge to blink them away. If she opened her eyes now... The unseen gaze grew in intensity; the clasping hands gripped hers tighter in excitement.

"What do you want?" she whispered, her voice cracking. It didn't answer, but she felt it lean closer. She swallowed, trying to moisten her dry throat.

"Please..." A sob threatened to break out of her chest. The icy fingers burned her hands; it was painful and unrelenting. She winced and a tear ran down her cheek, oddly hot against her chilled skin. Her head began to spin, like she was about to sink into the chasm of blackness that surrounded her.

She felt the change in the air as it drew closer, felt its frosty breath as it leaned in hungrily towards her. The pain in her fingers was unbearable, but this unending moment was even more so.

Slowly it swooped, moving closer to her face, which tensed as she recoiled, her jaw rigid and her lips clamped tightly shut. Closer it came, and she could sense the smile on its face. *Closer...* The sweat trickled down her back; her heart fluttered as if it wanted to take off and fly far away. Her chest ached with the effort of staying still and silent. *Closer...*

Stone-cold lips kissed the tear on her cheek.

Her gasp of surprise was matched by its sigh of satisfaction. It had what it wanted. After one last, triumphant squeeze, the cold fingers released her numb hands.

The rich, mouldering scent faded gradually away as the air warmed. The heaviness in her limbs lifted and she flopped slightly, her hands falling onto her lap. She flexed her fingers carefully; they felt stiff and bruised. Cautiously, she opened her eyes.

The room was empty. She knew this because the moon shone from behind her, lighting up the toys in the construction area. She knew it because the light from her classroom beamed through the glass panel. She knew it because the heavy atmosphere had lifted as the cold had receded.

She stayed there a moment, hunched on the ground, her mind racing as she replayed the events of the last few minutes. Her trembling fingers pressed against the burning cold spot on her left cheek, the butterflies swarmed, and suddenly she could take it no more.

She scrambled to her feet and stumbled to the door, yanking it open and racing through. She swept up her bag and keys and flew through her classroom, into the corridor, and out of the main entrance.

She didn't stop to set the alarm, nor did she lock the door. She didn't even close the gate as she hurried to her car. She unlocked it, jumped inside, switched on the headlights and started the engine, revving the accelerator as she sped away from what was behind her.

The lights in the school blazed reproachfully in her rear-view mirror.

She knew there would be questions, later. People would want to know why she had been so irresponsible, why she had left so suddenly, why she would never go back. She knew there would be consequences.

But the memory of that ice-cold kiss wiped all of those concerns away. She would deal with them another day. Right here, right now, there was only one thing to do.

She pressed her foot firmly on the accelerator pedal and sped towards home.

The dark country lanes twisted as she raced along them, barely needing to even look as she flew along the dyke-lined route she had travelled so many times before. Her mind was miles away, back at the old building and the thing that she had experienced there. She remembered again how she was always the last to leave; perhaps now she understood why.

She glanced in the rear-view mirror; the school was far behind her, but the chill had followed. She realised she was gripping the steering wheel tightly, and shook her hands, one at a time, to loosen her stiff fingers.

She forced her shoulders to relax and stretched her hand out to turn up the heating. Her eyes left the road briefly as she turned the dial to its maximum setting. The hot air blasted onto her face, feeling painful on her cold skin. She adjusted the fan and let it blow gently over her hands until they began to feel warmer.

She eased off the accelerator, sat back in her seat and began to feel calmer; the butterflies stilled and her heart resumed beating normal time.

She shook her head in wonder as she continued along the narrow lane, heading for the main road and home. Already, she felt silly. She imagined trying to explain what had happened and, even to her, it sounded ridiculous. Who would believe her tale? The weight of unfulfilled responsibility was heavy on her shoulders. If anything happened at the unlocked school that night she'd lose her job.

She contemplated pulling over and phoning the caretaker, but dismissed that idea as she tried and failed to imagine a plausible-sounding excuse for leaving the school unlocked. The further she travelled, the more she began to regret her hasty exit. She sighed at the realisation: she would have to go back, and she would have to go back alone.

At the precise moment that thought entered her mind, a cold sigh whispered on her left cheek. She jerked her head up and stared into the rear-view mirror. Staring back at her were a pair of piercing blue eyes, so like her own, but these were not wide with fear as she was sure hers must be. They held her with their gaze, bright and hard in a face whose shape suggested youth, even as it was lined with age.

She screamed as it smiled at her in the mirror, the sound muffled by the car's soft interior.

She saw the bend too late, turned the wheel too hard, felt the car pitch down and into the dyke. The thing behind her giggled as the airbag exploded with an ear-splitting bang, pinning her against the seat as the car thumped to a halt.

It rocked gently for a moment before the twinkling lights and butterflies in her head spun her into unconsciousness.

When she awoke, the first thing she knew was that she was alive. The pain in her chest from the seatbelt's tight grip was too real to be imagined, as was the sulphurous smell of the air-bag, deflated now like a forgotten party balloon.

She winced as she unbuckled her seatbelt; she'd cracked a rib, possibly, but her arms and legs seemed fine. She shoved the car door open, hissing a breath between her teeth at the jarring pain in her chest, and clambered out of the car and up the bank.

Her car looked forlorn, its nose lost in weeds and water. The rear lights shone bravely: the only light besides the moon, which cast an eerie glow over the deserted marsh road. Few cars ever passed by here. No one would have found her for hours.

As she realised how close she'd come to disaster, her legs buckled and gave way, and she sobbed into her palms where she sat, howling with a mixture of hysteria and relief.

Her cries carried across the marsh, scaring birds and small creatures who fled from the keening sound. Her chest heaved and her tears fell in hot streams on her face and hands until she thought she would drown in them.

Eventually though, the sobbing slowed to a sniffle and she became suddenly aware of the cold. She raised her head and wiped her cheeks with her sleeve, pulling her coat around her more tightly against the harsh wind. She shuddered as the memory of that child-creature's kiss returned. It had been in her car, staring at her in the mirror, before she'd crashed.

She jumped to her feet, her legs wobbling slightly like a new-born calf as she found her balance.

Where was it now? She scanned the horizon quickly but could see no sign of it- or of any rescuer.

Holding on to weeds and tufts of long grass, she half-stepped, half-slid, back towards her car. She reached inside and turned off the engine; the lights died so that only the moonlight remained to illuminate the scene. The same moon that shone through the window a few minutes- hours- ago? She didn't know how long she'd been unconscious; it had been dark already as she'd left- dark for a long time. Who knew what time it was now?

An image pushed itself into her head: her dogs, waiting patiently for her at home, sat in the window with their tails wagging. Tears pricked her eyelids once more- she wanted to be there. She'd never wanted anything so much as she wanted her sofa, slippers and dogs right now. She shivered in the cold night air and longed for a cup of tea. Tea always made things better.

But there was no tea here. Here, there was only herself and her crashed car, useless in the dyke. She leaned across the driver's seat for her handbag- maybe her phone would have some signal so she could call someone to pick her up. Emma would come. Emma wouldn't laugh at her.

The cracked screen told her it was 8:17pm, but otherwise only confirmed her fears- no signal. She never could get decent reception, this far out in the Fens. She tapped the buttons hopefully but was not surprised that the call to her friend didn't connect.

She shoved the phone into her coat pocket; useless as it was, she still couldn't bear to let it go. She wriggled awkwardly back out of the car and turned to climb back up the bank, her cars keys jangling sadly in her right hand.

It was waiting for her there at the top of the bank, lit from the side as if by a spotlight. Somehow she'd known it would be, but she still froze in shock at the sight of it.

It was smaller than she had imagined through her tightly-shut eyes, back in Class 1; the body was child-sized and frail, the clothes rough and ill-fitting, as if they were hand-me-downs from an earlier time.

Its short, white hair seemed to absorb the moonlight, rather than reflect it, giving it an unreal quality like a badly super-imposed special effect in a cheap horror film.

They stared at each other for a moment, the teacher and the child, and she realised with a jolt that that was indeed what it looked like- a child. Its face was weathered and lined, giving it a wizened appearance but its eyes were young and soft. It looked... vulnerable.

It raised a hand towards her and she backed away in

confusion, pressing herself against the car, which rocked slightly. She couldn't run. There was nowhere to run to. She considered getting back into the car and locking the doors, waiting for daylight, but the idea of huddling there, surrounded by black windows, waiting for it to appear at one, was even more terrifying than facing it right now.

She fixed her eyes on it, determined to keep it in view. It turned its palm up and curled its fingers gently. She realised what it meant. It beckoned her with snow-white fingertips and a shy smile- so unlike the one she had imagined when her eyes were closed.

She took a small step up the bank. It waited, patiently. She took another. The fingertips twitched again and the smile broadened in encouragement.

She wasn't afraid- just numb, and not entirely from the biting gusts that had swept up the clouds and hurried them away, leaving the sky clear and full of stars.

"Who are you?" she asked, surprised at the bold sound of her voice. The figure answered with a smile, before turning away and disappearing from view over the crest of the bank. She jiggled from foot to foot, torn between curiosity and fear. Curiosity won, and she clambered slowly up the bank, her chest aching from the cold.

She was breathless when she reached the top. She looked hopefully for lights across the flat fields and marshes, but they were as dull and featureless as she had expected. She spun slowly in a complete circle, just to be sure. Nothing.

A prickle of flesh alerted her to its presence once more. She half-turned to her right. It stood less than a metre from her, where it had not been seconds before.

Its sapphire-coloured eyes gazed calmly up into hers. She realised, now she was closer, that its face was not old, but streaked with mud and dust. The soft jawline and delicate cheekbones were almost hidden under a layer of filth.

She could only guess, from the short hair, that the apparition was that of a small boy, maybe seven or eight years old. He looked sweet, not unlike some of the boys in her class. His eyes twinkled as if he had read her thoughts and he raised his hand once more, curling it around her fingers. It didn't feel so cold this time. She wondered vaguely if this was because he was warmer, or because she was colder.

He tugged insistently on her hand and, this time, she didn't even try to resist. He led her down the bank where the water was shallower and up the other side.

"Where are we going?" she asked. He didn't answer, just gave a shy half-smile and pulled her onwards. She followed willingly, the surreality of the situation taking away any fear. So many strange things had happened to her tonight that she had given up questioning now. Part of her even wondered if they had happened at all, or if she was, in fact, asleep with her head resting on a pile of unmarked books back in her classroom.

She let herself be led along a footpath running beside a hedge, and through a gap into a field. The land stretched ahead like an endless canvas, painted in a limited palate of greys. Her eyes, too used to bright lights and small rooms, struggled to make out any features or landmarks.

She concentrated on watching where she placed her feet instead, her chin tucked into the collar of her coat for warmth as he led her on.

They walked in silence through the stubby remains of crops. He strode purposefully, looking back every few minutes at her face as if to gauge her reaction. She returned his smile, which seemed to grow more excited each time their eyes met. They didn't need to speak, not that this strange child-creature seemed capable of it, and she didn't ask any more questions; it was clear that wherever they were going, it was going to be a surprise.

With the same resignation to her fate as she had felt in the classroom, but without the terror, she let herself be steered towards their unknown destination.

Every so often, they would cross a dyke. He knew the best places to cross, and led her carefully down and back up the banks, his hand never leaving hers.

Where the valley was too wide to jump over the water, he led her along to an earth bridge. He moved instinctively, through habit, and she wondered how he knew the land so well- had he lived here once? He walked the route like he had been doing it for many years, sure-footed and confident.

Maybe this was the way he had walked when he was alive. Maybe this was the way he walked every night now. She had no doubt that he was a ghost- so many things tonight had proved that to her- but she was not afraid now. He was just a child.

She studied the back of his head as they walked; his hair was cut neatly, although it was ruffled and wavy, as if it had dried in the wind while damp. It was strange how it didn't move in the icy breeze and seemed to glow slightly- a luminescence that reminded her of old photographs she had seen.

She tried to guess when he had lived. His trousers were rolled up at the ankle and his jumper had patches on the elbows: this made her smile. It seemed such an odd detail for her mind to focus on, with everything that had happened so far this night. His clothes were not modern, but she couldn't pin them down to a specific time. No clues there, then.

She wondered how much further they had to go. The incessant wind was bitter and she was chilled despite their brisk pace. He didn't appear to tire, moving silently through the fields, almost at her side, but still leading the way with a dogged determination.

She guessed they had been trudging for miles already, though it was hard to judge, and the dull ache in her chest had begun to throb with the effort of keeping up, each ragged breath filling her lungs with fire.

She was weak from the cold and the pain; she couldn't walk much further without a rest. Pulling on his hand, she planted her feet to stop his momentum carrying her forward.

"Please, can we stop for a minute?"

He paused and looked up at her, concern on his small face. He pointed into the distance, his eyes pleading with her to continue. Not far now they seemed to say.

"Are we nearly there?"

He nodded, his eyes flashing as he squeezed her hand reassuringly. She couldn't resist him, and the part of her that wasn't slowly freezing to death wanted to know what was so important, so vital, that he had chosen her and nearly killed her so she could see it. She needed to know, needed to solve the mystery.

She sighed and set off once more, her muscles feeling stiff. She hoped there would be tea at the end of this.

They walked in silence for a few more minutes. Her eyes had adjusted to the darkness now; she could make out the shape of the land in the soft moonlight. No sound disturbed the night except for her steady footsteps and the rustle of her clothes as she moved. Even the nocturnal creatures were hushed and still.

The lazy wind blew straight through her, making her teeth chatter. She was so cold that the tiny hand in hers began to feel warm. She clung to it for support, taking comfort from its confident lead across the grey fields.

Ahead, in the distance, she thought she could see cheerful

lights glowing. A house? The child pointed again; this was clearly their destination, although the darkness made it difficult to perceive exactly how far away it might be.

Her spirits lifted at the prospect of light, warmth, and people. Maybe he felt guilty for causing the crash and was leading her to safety. She certainly wouldn't have found her way back to civilisation until daylight- if she'd have lasted that long on this cold night. Her pace quickened slightly as she used her limited energy reserves to push forward towards the light.

She struggled on until they reached a deep dyke, wider than the others they had crossed. She looked to the child, waiting for him to show her which way to go now, but he was motionless. He stared across the deep valley at the distant house, his lip trembling slightly.

"Is this what you wanted to show me?" she asked. He glanced up at her, his eyes bright, before returning to face the house. She followed his gaze. The house was small, more like a cottage, and the light that had seemed like a beacon was only the chinks that escaped through gaps in the curtains of a downstairs room.

"Well, let's go then," she urged, a trace of school-teacher returning to her tone. He shook his head sadly and pointed to a heap of wood partially submerged in the deep water. She took a tentative step forward to inspect it more closely. It wasn't a collection of rubbish, washed up and wedged into position. Some pieces were joined together, the planks still nailed to posts by rusting nails.

"Was this a bridge?"

He nodded, and pointed again at the house on the other bank. It was close enough that she imagined she could hear soft music and smell smoke from a log fire. Surely, if she shouted, someone would hear her? They couldn't give up now- not when they'd come so far.

She edged her toes over the crest of the bank, meaning to slide down and cross. He pulled her back, eyes wide in fear. He shook his head urgently, pointing at the black water before raising his hand high above his head.

"It's deep? Too deep for you?"

He nodded, pleased she understood.

"Well, it might not be too deep for me. I'm taller than you."

He jumped, holding his hand up over her head. She assessed the dyke again, squinting into the darkness. The distance between the visible banks was wider than any she'd seen tonight, which suggested the murky water was deeper too. She chewed on her lip while she tried to think of a solution. Her lip was so cold she couldn't feel her teeth gnawing on them.

He was staring at the house again, a desperately longing expression on his small face. *Think*, she urged herself. She looked left and right for another way to cross, but could find none. If there had been another, she reasoned, he would have taken her to it. This was obviously a place he didn't know how to cross. She wondered how long he had been trying for.

"Is there another way?" she asked, just in case. "A road?" He shrugged his shoulders and shook his head. He didn't know. Maybe the layout of the area had changed, since he… This was obviously the only way he knew, and now he didn't know how to cross. She wondered how long he had been trying for.

She contemplated the muddy water. It looked cold. *Can't go round it*, she sang in her head. *Can't go over it*. She knew what she had to do, and she wasn't going to enjoy it. *Got to go through it*, she decided silently, shuddering at the prospect but knowing it was necessary. She turned to face him.

STRANGE IDEAS: DEATH, DESTINY AND DECISIONS

"We could swim?"

He shook his head sadly.

"You can't swim?"

He looked down, embarrassed, and nodded.

"Well, luckily for you, I can."

He raised his head quickly, lifting his eyebrows in a silent question. She knelt down and led him around her in a circle, his hand held tight in hers still, until he was stood behind her. Her arm was crossed across her chest, she would have to swim using only one. She hoped she had the strength left for this final challenge.

"Hold onto me," she instructed, trying her hardest to sound calm and authoritative. He responded to her tone, and wrapped his other arm around her neck.

"Not too tight," she laughed. He shifted his arm so that he wasn't hurting her. She stood slowly, lifting his feather-weight easily but struggling to push her tired legs up from the floor. She really hoped she could do this.

She took a deep, painful, breath and slid awkwardly down the bank, using her free hand to hold onto tufts of grass and slow her descent.

Despite her care, she lost her footing as they reached the edge of the water and was suddenly plunged up to her waist. The effect was astonishing: her legs locked rigid and she gasped in pain, her chest constricting in shock. How could it be so cold? She hadn't expected it to feel warm- she wasn't stupid- but she'd hoped that the fact that she was practically hypothermic already would mean she didn't feel it quite so much. The water was actually hurting her, burning her skin like acid. It was excruciating. Uncontrollable spasms shuddered through her body and she panted as she tried and failed to move her legs forward.

The child's hand squeezed hers; it was the only comfort

and encouragement he could give her, but it was enough. Thank goodness the other bank was only a few metres away. She lowered herself into the icy water, hissing at the pain and trying not to think about the phone still in her pocket. She began to swim.

The freezing temperature of the water sapped her strength and it took a supreme effort to kick her legs. The child was no weight at all, but the loss of one arm meant that she struggled to keep afloat and moving forward at all.

She imagined Mediterranean oceans and bubble baths, gritting her teeth against the body-shaking convulsions, and ploughed on. The bank was in shadow and difficult to see; her arm ached like she had been swimming for hours already and yet it was still no closer.

She gasped for breath, trying not to inhale the black water by mistake; she was frightened now, more frightened than she had been when the car had dived off the road, more frightened even than when she had been on her knees in the darkness, dreading the thing that trapped her. How silly she had been, how superstitious. He was only a child. He needed her help, and she had run away from him. She wouldn't fail him now- not when they had come so far together.

This thought spurred her on, and a final few kicks brought her to the opposite bank, her precious load still clinging safely to her back. She climbed out of the water, feeling dangerously warm now she had left its icy chill behind, and scrambled up to the top. She collapsed to her knees and let the boy slide from her back. He danced around her, still holding her hand, until he stood at her side again, looking down at her white face.

She was exhausted. The lights from the house blurred before her eyes and she blinked and rubbed them as she struggled to her feet. The child helped her, surprisingly strong

STRANGE IDEAS: DEATH, DESTINY AND DECISIONS

for his size, and she stumbled forward. He sped up, almost dragging her behind him, so strong was his desire to reach the house. She put all her strength into keeping up with him, her legs screaming in agony with each heavy footstep.

The child was almost skipping now, tugging at her hand as he raced towards the house. He looked over his shoulder at her, a huge grin across his face. The effect was magical. She laughed and ran with him, her aches and stiffness suddenly forgotten as his infectious joy overwhelmed her.

They reached the front door of the house and she threw herself against it, knocking as hard as her feeble arms would allow. She heard shuffling steps behind the door before it opened a crack and a wrinkled face peered out. Before she could even speak, the door was opened wide, the welcome heat flooding over her shivering limbs.

"Oh, my dear! Whatever has happened to you? Come inside, quick; you look half-frozen!"

She was ushered inside by an old woman, straight into a cosy sitting room. As she had supposed, a log fire blazed cheerfully, but she sat away from it on a couch, nearly disappearing into the upholstery. A radio was playing in the background. The old woman disappeared from sight briefly, returning with a towel from the kitchen.

"Now, dear," the old woman said. "Get those wet things off while I fetch you some dry clothes. You look like you've been swimming in a dyke."

She couldn't help it: she began to giggle. The absurdity of swimming in a dyke in October! She peeked over at the child and saw he was grinning too. The woman, unsure of the joke, nevertheless smiled politely as she backed out of the room.

She managed to stop laughing long enough to kick off her shoes and rub the towel roughly over her face and hair, and was calm again by the time the woman returned with clothes and blankets.

Casting modesty aside, she stripped off her wet clothes and pulled on the dry ones, her hand leaving his only for the time it took to thrust her arms down the sleeves of a woollen jumper with patches on the sleeves.

She placed her phone on the arm of the couch, in the small hope that it might recover from its dip in the dyke.

The old woman bustled around her, wrapping her in the hurriedly fetched blankets from the airing cupboard. They were uncomfortably warm on her skin, but the burning tingle was a relief after the many hours of cold followed by the icy swim.

"I'll get you something hot- some tea. No- don't move. Time enough to tell me what happened after you've warmed up." The woman left the room again.

She heard the sound of a kettle being filled, and sank back gratefully on the over-stuffed couch. Closing her eyes, she wriggled her toes as the numbness melted away and the feeling returned to them. The soft music floated around her and enveloped her in a cocoon of pleasant melody.

What would she tell the woman? Certainly not the truth- she'd never believe it. She wasn't sure she believed it herself, not now she was back in the normal world. If it wasn't for the fact that the child's fingers were still wrapped in hers, she'd think she had imagined the whole thing. Were hallucinations a symptom of hypothermia?

She felt, rather than saw, his eyes roaming over her face. She opened her eyes. He was sat next to her, gazing at her adoringly. She smiled, and he smiled back. She closed her eyes again, his hand nestled in her own.

The woman returned, carrying a tea tray with cups, saucers and a teapot complete with knitted cosy.

"Now, that's better," the old woman said, placing the tray

on a low table and hanging the already-steaming clothes over the clothes-horse by the fire before pouring the tea. "I'm Mabel, by the way. You'd better tell me how you got in this state. I can't imagine what you've been up to!"

She told Mabel an edited version of her evening- working late, losing control of the car, stumbling across fields for miles- and the woman oohed and tutted sympathetically in all the right places, pouring more tea and adding more sugar as the tale was told.

"And then I saw your lights, swam the dyke and scared you half to death by banging on your door in the middle of the night!" she ended, taking another long drink of her tea.

"Well, what a lot of bad luck you've had! And the chances of you finding me here- there's only me and Ted down the road for miles this way." Mabel shuddered. "You might have frozen out there, soaking wet on a night like this. Doesn't bear thinking about. Still, we'll have you sorted right enough. Ted down the road has a car and I'm sure he won't mind driving you home. I'll ring and ask him- he won't mind. Will you be able to find your car in the morning?"

"Oh, yes. It'll be hard to miss in daylight."

"Good. I'll go and telephone him in a bit. Are you warming up now?"

"Lovely, thank you." She looked around the room properly for the first time. The room was decorated in an old-fashioned style, or maybe just hadn't been decorated in a while, but it was clean and cosy. Every available surface was covered in mismatched photo frames, souvenirs and ornaments: a library of memories spanning many years. The effect was comforting, like being surrounded by silent, smiling friends.

"You have a beautiful home," she said. "Just lovely."

"Bless you!" Mabel blushed, her powdery-white skin

warming to a pretty shade of pink. "It's easy to keep tidy when you're on your own, even if I'm not so energetic with the cleaning as I was. It's been six years since my George passed and, although I miss him every day, I don't miss chasing him round the house, picking up his newspapers and such." She laughed fondly. "Never knew anyone so terrible for making a mess and leaving things in strange places."

She leaned over and picked up a photo frame from the side table, pointing out a tall man with sandy-blond hair. "That's him. That was taken not long after we'd moved here, in 1946."

"1946? You've lived here all that time? You must really love this house."

"Yes. It was our first and only home together." She smiled at the memory. "We raised our children here, watched them grow, and watched them leave to find their own way." She stood up and crossed the room to collect another photo. She stroked the glass tenderly before handing it over. "That's all of us. Helen at the back, next to George, William, and little Matthew on my knee." She pointed to each one in turn.

The photo had been taken in front of the house on a bright, summer day. Mabel looked very young, dressed in her Sunday-best with a wriggling toddler wrapped tightly in her arms as she perched on a tree stump. George stood proudly behind her, holding the hand of a little girl with angelic curls and a self-conscious smile. The older boy, William, sat cross-legged next to his mother, squinting at the camera and beaming widely. The sun smiled down on them all; it was a happy family portrait.

She leaned forward to study their faces more carefully. Helen obviously took after her mother, and there was a similarity already between Matthew's little face and his father's; they shared the same nose. She looked again at

William, grinning cheerfully into the camera lens. He looked like a typical boy, sitting nicely for a photo but yearning to be off playing as soon as possible. He gave the impression that he was about to sprint away into the fields and build a fort or climb a tree.

She peered at his face. There was something in his smile that seemed familiar. The picture was old and slightly out-of-focus- she supposed technology had moved on leaps and bounds since this was taken- but there was enough detail in his features for her to recognise him.

A gentle squeeze on her hand confirmed her suspicions. She peeked over at him. He was staring at the photo with a look of intense joy on his face. He raised his eyes to hers, and they shone with tears, despite the wide beam on his lips. He nodded. She understood. She knew now why he had brought her here.

"Mabel," she began, handing the photo back with a trembling hand. "Tell me about your children."

Mabel took the photo and laid it in her lap. She was silent for a moment, her head bowed.

"Well, Matthew, my youngest, is an accountant in Kings Lynn. He did very well for himself," she added proudly, lifting her chin. "My daughter-in-law doesn't have to work- not like these poor women you read about who have to keep up with a job and running a home- and they come over with my grand-children and their children to see me every couple of months. Helen moved to Australia after she married and she and her husband run a restaurant together in Perth. They visit every Christmas."

She sighed. "It's hard, her being so far away, but she's happy there." She fiddled with the photo, unsure of how to continue, her loneliness filling the silence.

"And... William?"

"Oh, William." She sighed deeply, and a shadow of sorrow passed over her face. "William died the winter after that photo was taken. He was only just seven. He was still a baby." Her eyes grew dark at the memory. "It was in the flood. I'm sure you've heard about it? There was a lot on the television about it awhile back, marking the anniversary." She shook her head. "As if any of us could ever forget it."

She remembered seeing it on the news. The Great Flood of 1953. Hundreds had been drowned or died from exposure that terrible night. Back in the days before telephone alerts or sirens, there had been no warning, no chance to escape the great swathes of icy black water that raced across the flat Fens into people's homes. There had been memorial services all over Lincolnshire. She had taken some children to one, as representatives from the school.

"What happened to him?"

Mabel's face screwed into a grimace. "It was all the dog's fault." She laughed, bitterly. "George had found him a puppy for his birthday- he was doo-lally about animals, wanted to be a vet when he grew up- and we couldn't disappoint him, even though money was so tight then. He loved that dog, spent all day playing in the fields with him, saved him scraps from the table and even hid him under his jumper so he could take him up to bed at night." She stroked the smiling face in the photo, so full of life and mischief. "He thought we didn't know about that."

Guilt brought colour to her cheeks. The memory was clearly painful for the old woman, but she needed to know. He'd found her, brought her here for a reason. Feeling awful, she asked anyway.

"How did he die?"

Mabel took a deep breath. "The floods came in the night, when we were all tucked up in bed. William had been out with George that day, walking the dog across the marshes and looking for birds' eggs. I remember telling him off because he was covered in mud up to his thighs. I asked him if he'd been rolling in it, and George said that the tide must be high because the ground was so boggy where they were- that he'd fallen in soft patches a few times. He said it was unusual for the water to be so far inland but I didn't pay any attention- I was more worried about how I was going to get all that muck out: it was too late to start any washing and I had enough work to do the next day.

"William and the dog were even worse. I stripped him off and got him in the tub, and told him the dog had to stay outside. He cried and argued that it was too cold, but I was cross and wouldn't listen. I wish I had now." Her lip trembled at the memory.

"I woke up that night to Matthew's crying and, when I went downstairs to fetch his clean clothes that I'd left drying by the fire, I saw the water lapping at the door. I was terrified. I shouted up to George. He looked out of the window and said the dyke had burst and to get back upstairs. He was a brave man but I heard fear in his voice that night, though he tried hard to hide it from us.

"He came down to try and block up the doors and stop the water coming in. By this time, the children were all awake. William was pulling on his clothes as he ran down the stairs and Helen had followed William because she was frightened to be alone in the dark- she was only four. I took her back up to our bedroom and tucked her up under the blankets, told her it would all be alright. Matthew was already in there anyway, and was screaming his little heart out because he was wet and cold. I changed his clothes as quickly as I could and then went to look for William. He hadn't followed me when I'd brought Helen back upstairs. I thought he was helping

George. It was all so confusing- such a panic." She took a sip of her tea before continuing. Her cup rattled as she placed it back on the saucer.

"I called down to George to ask if William was with him, but he said no. I ran back into the children's bedroom to check, but he was gone." She looked up, guilt and regret etched into the lines on her face. "He'd gone out to look for his dog, dressed in the dirty clothes he'd been wearing that day- he hadn't even taken his coat. I suppose he couldn't bear to think of the poor animal out there in all that water. He was soft about that dog.

"George went out to look for them, but it was dark, and the water was rising higher. It was so fast. I've never seen anything like it. From the bedroom window, it seemed like we were looking out onto the North Sea itself, with roofs and tree-tops instead of ships and islands. I was frantic, waiting for George and William to come back. Helen was sobbing and Matthew, baby as he was, knew that something wasn't right and wouldn't stop screaming. I rocked him and paced for what felt like hours, but he wouldn't settle. I wonder now if he knew somehow- that William was drowned. He couldn't swim, you see?"

Her eyes began to fill with tears, but she seemed to need to continue.

"When George eventually returned, cradling a soaked and frightened dog but no William, I screamed at him to go back and find his son." She was weeping openly now. "He said to me that it was too dangerous, the water was too deep and the current too strong. We sat up all night, the four of us and the dog huddled together in that small room, until dawn came. As the hours crept by, I prepared myself for the worst. It was terrible out there, and poor little William- he was only a child, and he couldn't even swim. He didn't have a chance."

STRANGE IDEAS: DEATH, DESTINY AND DECISIONS

A teardrop fell onto the photo she clutched in her hands.

"At first light, George went straight out to look for William- but I knew he wouldn't be able to bring him back.

"They found his body a few miles away, when the waters receded enough to explore, a couple of days later. He's buried not far from here. I'll never forgive myself. I should have let that dog sleep inside, like William asked, but I was too worried about clearing up the mess. He was such a good boy, so sweet, never one to let a living creature suffer."

She fell into silence, her tale told.

All the time his mother had been speaking, William had sat motionless but now he rose from the couch, an anguished look on his face as he witnessed her grief. He reached over to the sobbing woman and took her hands in his, kneeling before her as if in worship.

She gasped at his touch and looked up, confused. Now was the right time to explain.

"Mabel," she began, unsure of the right words, "I don't think I came here tonight by accident. I think that somehow William found me and brought me here, that he needed me to help him find his way home to you. He's here now. He's holding your hands. Can you feel him?"

Mabel's eyes moved away, flicking to her hands before lifting again and focussing on the figure before her. He seemed to solidify under her gaze, filling with light and warmth, until he glowed like the sun. The two women watched, speechless, as his sandy hair became golden, his eyes sparkled with love and his lips filled with fire.

Mabel's eyes widened in wonder and the tears ran down her cheeks as she recognised the face of the son she had lost over sixty years ago.

"Yes, I can see him! William! My darling little boy! I'm so sorry, so terribly sorry." She held his hands to her lips and kissed them, ran her fingers over his delicate features and stared adoringly at his face. She tore her eyes away to look at the woman who had brought him home. "How did you..? How is this possible?"

"I don't know. All I know is that he tried so hard to make me listen, wanted so desperately to come home to you. I don't think he blames you at all; he's just so glad to be with you again. He couldn't do it on his own- he needed me to help him. I think he's been trying to come home for a long time."

She told Mabel the full ghostly tale, only leaving out the part where she had initially been so repulsed by him back in the school that she had tried to abandon him and flee. She was ashamed of that now. William smiled understandingly; he wouldn't tell.

"It's a miracle! My William!" Mabel released his hands and wiped her eyes with a handkerchief, pulled hastily from her sleeve. "I can't thank you enough. You've brought my little boy home, after all these years." She blew her nose noisily.

William turned to look at the woman who had helped him, gratitude shining from his smile. He reached out and took her hand; his skin was warm, like sun-kissed sand on a beach. She treasured the feel of his touch; how strange, when she had feared it so much before. That was before she knew him. He was just a child: a lost, lonely child, searching for someone to help him find his way home.

Home. She remembered who was waiting for her there: her dogs, her family and her friends. She had fulfilled her task; she had solved the mystery; she had helped reunite mother and child. It was time to go.

"Mabel?" She spoke softly. "Would it be alright if you asked Ted about taking me home now?" Mabel sat up, poking her handkerchief back into her sleeve.

STRANGE IDEAS: DEATH, DESTINY AND DECISIONS

"Oh, my dear! Please forgive me! After everything you've done for me and William... I almost forgot... I'll telephone him now." She rose, still sniffing, and stepped out into the hallway, taking a last look to check that William was still there. He waved at her, letting her know he was here to stay now. She smiled sweetly back at him, a smile filled with love, before she disappeared out of view. Her voice was low as she spoke to Ted-down-the-road on the landline.

In the sitting room, she and William, teacher and child, waited in silence. She held his hand and gazed at his face, wondering what he was thinking. How must it feel, to have been away and alone for so long? She wanted to cry at the thought of it. All those years of trying to find someone who would listen, the desperation building until he had been forced to extreme measures. How many times had he been ignored? How many people had run from his cold touch? And Mabel, blaming herself, longing for one more chance to say goodbye, alone in her little cottage with all her family gone.

She smiled. They were together again now. Mabel returned to the sitting room.

"Ted down the road says he's on his way and won't be long. He wasn't in bed yet." She wrung her hands awkwardly. "I didn't tell him about... about William coming home. I don't know how I'll explain that to anyone."

"Yes. I can see how it might be difficult." The two women looked at William, then back at each other, before laughing together like old friends sharing an inside-joke. She stood and gathered her clothes from the clothes-horse, bundling them into a ball and tucking them under her arm. "I'll wash and return the clothes you've lent me," she started to say. Mabel interrupted her, waving her words away with flapping hands.

"Now, don't you worry about that," she scolded. "There's no need at all. Unless, of course, you'd like to come back for a cup of tea one day?" William nodded his agreement.

"I'd love to! I'd be fascinated to hear all about your life here. Thank you." Her smile was genuine, as was her acceptance of the offer. Mabel needed some company, and she would be glad to chat some more with her.

She slipped her feet back into her shoes, which were still damp but were nicely warmed from the fire. "If it's ok, I'll wait for Ted outside. Give you some time with William." William jumped up and looked to his mother for permission. Mabel laughed again.

"I rather think he wants to see you out." She smiled fondly at him. "Go on, see the nice lady to the car. We've got all the time we want together now."

She stepped forward to embrace Mabel before she left. Her eyes were shining again in happiness and wonder.

"Thank you," she whispered as she walked her to the door, William squeezing beside them both. "Thank you for bringing my little boy home."

"My pleasure." They embraced again before she stepped outside. William wrapped his hand in hers. Mabel, understanding that they needed to say their own goodbyes, waved and pulled the door partially closed, leaving them alone. The firelight spilled out and lit the doorstep as they walked, hand in hand, to the edge of the garden.

William turned towards her. His other hand caressed her shoulder, and she stooped down until they were face to face. She smiled into the child's face, matching his joy. This close, he smelt of warm milk and ripe apples, soft grass and sunlight.

How had she ever been afraid of him? Lit by the warm glow of firelight escaping through the open door, he looked like an angel.

He squeezed her shoulder gently before taking her empty hand, which tingled as the tiny fingers wrapped themselves around hers. She could feel his breath on her face; it tasted sweet, like morning dew. Her eyes were open. She wanted to remember every second of this, their time together.

Her eyes pricked with tears and she let them flow softly down her cheeks. His brow furrowed with concern; his hands gripped hers tighter in alarm.

"It's ok," she whispered, her voice cracking. "You're home now. You found her." He didn't answer, but nodded and smiled gratefully. It lit up his face like sunshine, and she could see clearly the little boy he once was, all those years ago when he had left his coat behind in the middle of the night.

She swallowed, trying to move the lump that had formed there. It was time to let him go.

"Goodbye..." A sob threatened to break out of her chest. Her fingers gripped his hands; this parting was bittersweet. A tear ran down her cheek, cool against her fire-warmed skin. Her head span with everything she had experienced that night, with the fear and cold and sorrow- and the miracle of seeing a child reunited with his mother.

She leaned in tenderly towards him, moving closer to his cherub-like face, which turned up eagerly to her, his eyes shining and his lips stretched in a beaming smile. The tears trickled down her cheek; the butterflies swarmed and broke free. Her chest ached with joy and relief.

The mystery was solved. He was home.

She kissed his blanket-soft cheek.

Her gasping sob was matched by his sigh of happiness. He had what he wanted. He was home with his mum; she had helped him find his way. After one last, triumphant squeeze, his fingers released hers and he stood. He skipped towards the front door, turned and waved, and then disappeared inside.

ABOUT THE AUTHOR

Louise West is an avid reader and music-lover, as well as being a sporadic blogger who fits everything in with full-time teaching and being pack leader to two dogs.

She is currently teaching and surviving in rural Lincolnshire, famed for its beautiful open sky and not much else. She dreams of rainy days and cups of tea. She and her faithful terriers love long walks on the beach, where they can bounce in the surf and she can paddle with her shoes on. She will only eat trifle if her Nan made it.
Sometimes she has Strange Ideas.
Sometimes she writes them down.

If you have enjoyed this collection, and would like to find out more about Louise West or her other Strange Ideas, then remember you can:

Visit the author online at:
www.louisesloveoflife.webs.com

www.strangeideas.webs.com

Check out her blog at:
www.louise-west.blogspot.com

Find her on Facebook:
www.facebook.com/LouiseWestWriter

or follow her on Twitter
www.twitter.com/louisewest24

Reviews on Amazon, Goodreads or anywhere else (excluding bathroom walls) are always welcome and appreciated.